Sweet Silence

I.M. Knight

Misfit Horror
Published by Misfit Pages
Texas USA

On the World Wide Web at www.misfitpages.com

First Published 2026

Cover by Getcovers

ISBN: 9781962613293

DEDICATION

For my sister, whose reaction to my initial twisted dream concept made it all the more unsettling. Thank you for confirming that, yes, it *is* that creepy.

The fluorescent tube above booth six had been flickering for three minutes, and Carter Jameson was the only one who noticed.

Not because the others were unobservant. Evan had his laptop cracked open at the edge of the table, running signal diagnostics on a map of Acacia Springs he'd pinned to three browser tabs. Maddie's tablet threw blue light across her glasses while she scrolled through something dense with footnotes. Derek was halfway through his second plate of fries. Ava had commandeered a stack of paper napkins and was sketching with a ballpoint pen she'd stolen from the waitress's apron, her dark eyes focused somewhere past the paper. And Riley—

Riley was tracing the edge of her coffee mug with one finger, her other hand resting on the table with her wrist turned down. Hiding the tattoo. She always hid the tattoo.

Carter hadn't touched his coffee. He was too wired for caffeine, which was ironic, or maybe just fitting. The mug sat cooling between his elbows while he arranged his pitch in his head one more time, the way he'd arranged it in the mirror that morning, and in the shower, and at three a.m. staring at the ceiling with his phone playing back their subscriber count.

Twelve thousand. Down from eighteen. The algorithm had buried them three months ago and nothing. Not the lighthouse series, not the abandoned mall. Not even the railroad tunnel that Derek still wouldn't shut up about had clawed them back.

"Listen," Carter said, and the booth shifted. Not everyone looked up. Ava didn't. Riley didn't. But the air changed the way it always did when Carter started pitching, because Carter pitching was a weather event whether you wanted it or not. "I know the last three locations didn't hit. I know. But this one's different."

"You said that about the mall," Derek said through a fry.

"The mall didn't have a body count."

That got Ava's eyes up. Just for a second.

Carter pulled out his phone, swiped to the satellite image he'd screenshotted and cropped for exactly this moment. The Delightful Candy Co. spread across the screen like a bruise: massive brick complex, collapsed smokestack, parking lot being slowly eaten by kudzu. He slid it to the center of the table.

"Delightful Candy Company. Acacia Springs. Operational 1927 to 1963, when the whole thing shut down overnight. No warning, no severance, no explanation. Hundreds of workers showed up one morning and the doors were locked." He let that sit for a beat.

"The disappearances," Maddie said, not looking up from her tablet.

Carter blinked. "Yeah. How did you—"

"Seventeen employees between March and October 1963. Official reports list industrial accidents, but the incident reports were sealed by the county and never released under three separate FOIA requests." She pushed her glasses up. "The production output numbers for that period are also anomalous. They actually *increased* during the disappearances, which doesn't track with a reduced workforce unless you account for—"

"Maddie." Derek waved a fry at her. "Breathe."

"—sorry. It's just. The numbers are actually significant."

"The numbers are great," Carter said, pivoting back, trying to hold the room. "This place has everything. Real history, real disappearances, local legends, and nobody's done a proper investigation with modern equipment. The urban exploration community has a hundred shaky flashlight videos and nothing usable. We go in with Evan's full rig, multiple cameras, and proper audio. We're the first team to do this right."

Derek nodded, too quickly. "I'm in. Obviously."

"You already said you were in yesterday," Evan murmured from behind his laptop.

"I'm saying it again. For the group." Derek leaned back, the vinyl squealing under him. His hand drifted up to the scar above his eyebrow, then dropped. "Place doesn't scare me."

Ava's pen paused on the napkin. She tilted her head at Derek the way she did; that specific angle, like she was looking at him from a frame to the left of where everyone else saw. Then she went back to drawing.

Carter watched Riley. He couldn't help it. She was the hinge and they both knew it. Her finger had stopped tracing the mug. Her other hand pressed flat against the table, and he could just see the edge of the tattoo beneath her sleeve. That strange candy wrapper design in faded color that she never talked about and he'd never asked the right questions about.

"Riles?" He kept his voice easy. Warm. The voice that worked on camera.

She looked at him, and something in her expression was older than twenty-three. "My great-grandfather disappeared there in '63."

The booth went quiet.

"The official story was an accident." Riley's jaw tightened. "My grandma called it something else."

She didn't finish.

The pause that followed was the kind Carter lived for: raw, real, the sort of moment that made people stop scrolling. And before he could catch himself, before the better version of Carter Jameson could put a hand on his own mouth, he said: "That's incredible content."

The table flinched. Evan's typing stopped. Derek's chewing slowed. Maddie's mouth opened, then closed.

Riley just stared at him. Her hand moved to cover her wrist.

"I mean—" Carter started.

"I know what you mean." Flat. Not angry. Worse than angry.

Ava's phone buzzed against the table. The screen lit up, and for a half-second the notification was visible to anyone looking. A message from no contact, no app badge, just white text on black:

CandyMan_1963: We've been expecting you.

Ava's brow creased. She stared at the screen for two full seconds, then turned the phone face-down on the table and went back to her napkin without a word.

Nobody asked.

"Look," Carter said, reassembling himself, pivoting away from the damage, toward the horizon. "I'm saying this place *matters*. It matters to Riley, it matters to the community, and it's going to matter to our audience because it's real. That's what we've been missing. Something real."

He could hear how it sounded: half-rehearsed, a little desperate, the subscriber count bleeding through every word. But he believed it completely.

The light above the booth flickered hard. Once, twice, then a sustained brownout that dropped the fluorescent tube to a sick amber glow for three full seconds before it buzzed back to life. Carter glanced up, then around the diner. The other lights were fine. The counter, the pie case, the OPEN sign in the window. All were steady.

He made a mental note: *good b-roll if they're filming.*

"Okay, so—signal strength out there is actually workable," Evan said, turning his laptop around. "The cell tower coverage isn't great, but I can boost it with the portable repeater. Streaming should hold." He paused. "Probably."

"Probably," Derek echoed.

"Probably's fine," Carter said.

"My equipment's been doing something weird since yesterday, though." Evan said it casually. "Packet drops at regular intervals. I'm still working on it. Which is fine."

"The factory's been closed since '63," Maddie added, scrolling. "But the county power grid shows intermittent draws from the address as recently as—" She stopped. Pushed her glasses up. "2019. Which is actually significant because—"

"We can dig into the research on site," Carter said. He was losing the room to data and he needed bodies in a van. "What I need right now is a yes or a no. From everyone."

He looked around the table. Derek: already nodding, already performing. Evan: closing the laptop, which was his yes. Maddie: mouth working silently around a statistic she'd have to save for later, but her eyes were bright. That was a yes.

Ava said nothing. She was still drawing. Carter glanced at her napkin and saw an angular roofline. Industrial, sharp, with a smokestack that shouldn't have been familiar because he hadn't shown her the full architectural photos yet. Just the satellite shot. He almost said something, then didn't.

"Ava?"

"Hmm?" She looked up like she'd been somewhere else. "Oh. Yeah, I'm in. Obviously." A ghost of a smile. "You know I can't resist an empty building."

That left Riley.

The whole booth oriented toward her. She sat very still, and Carter watched her thumb press hard against the inside of her wrist where the candy wrapper tattoo sat under her sleeve. A habitual gesture. Years of practice.

"Yeah," Riley said quietly. "I'll go."

Carter exhaled. "Good. That's good. Tonight, then. We load the van at Evan's, hit the road by—"

"One condition." Riley's voice cut clean. "Whatever we find in there, you don't spin it. You don't turn it into a bit. If this is real—and Carter, I'm telling you right now it's going to be real—you show it straight."

"Absolutely," Carter said, already framing the shot.

A faint sweetness drifted through the booth; something warm and sugary, almost cloying. Carter's nose wrinkled. The pie case. Had to be. The burnt coffee smell had been sitting so heavy all afternoon that the sugar just hadn't cut through until now.

Except the pie case was behind him, and the sweetness was coming from the direction of the window.

He didn't think about it. He was already standing, already digging for his wallet.

Derek pulled the diner door open and the group filed out into the late afternoon. Evan cradled his laptop bag, Maddie was still scrolling, Ava tucked the napkin sketch into her jacket without looking at it. Riley last, shoulders slightly hunched, one hand pressed against her wrist.

They were loud in the parking lot. Performing normalcy for themselves and doing a decent job of it.

Carter hung back and lifted his phone. A test shot—the group walking across cracked asphalt toward their cars, golden hour light catching the dust they kicked up. Good framing. Natural. The kind of footage that opened a documentary when things went wrong.

✳✳✳

"—and we're getting signal," Evan said, not looking up from the laptop balanced on a stack of equipment cases. "Which is the good news."

Carter ducked under a cable Evan had strung between two light stands and nearly knocked a tripod into Riley's monitor array. The garage smelled like solder and concrete dust and the chemical tang of gear fresh out of packaging. Five screens glowed across the back wall, turning the whole space into something that looked like mission control if mission control operated out of a two-car residential unit with bad ventilation.

"What's the bad news?" Carter asked.

"I didn't say there was bad news."

"You said 'which is the good news.' That implies—"

"We're getting *better* signal than we should be at this address." Evan paused. His fingers stopped on the keyboard. "Significantly better."

Carter waited for the rest. It didn't come. Evan just stared at his readout for another beat, then typed something and moved on.

"Great," Carter said. "Strong signal, clean feed. That's what we need."

The pre-stream test was running on the main monitor. Camera two showed the garage interior in wide shot: the whiteboard on the back wall with its hand-drawn factory blueprint in red, blue, and green marker, the equipment cases stacked like Tetris pieces, Derek trying to mount a bodycam to his chest harness and getting the strap tangled. Camera one was Carter's A-cam, currently pointed at the floor. The feed was live to a private link. Test mode. Invite only.

Riley was on the far side of the garage, threading batteries into headlamps with mechanical efficiency. She hadn't spoken much since they'd arrived. Her eyes kept drifting to the whiteboard with the blueprint she and Maddie had roughed out from architectural records and satellite photos. Then her gaze snapped back to the batteries in her hands. Every time Carter caught her looking, she wasn't looking.

"Pre-stream chat's already active," Maddie said from her corner. She had her tablet propped against a toolbox, cross-referencing something on her phone simultaneously. "We've got... seven viewers on a private test link."

Carter's head turned. "Seven? Already?"

"Should be zero," Evan said quietly. He didn't look up.

"Could be bots. Or the link leaked." Maddie pushed her glasses up. "But the engagement pattern doesn't look automated. These accounts have viewing histories."

"That's organic interest," Carter said, and he felt the familiar spark that meant something was working, the algorithm might actually notice them this time. "That's good. This is already building."

He crossed to the main monitor and leaned in. The chat window was a thin column on the right side of the test feed. Mostly blank. A couple of messages:

StreamFan23: Is this the candy factory stream? When do you guys go live?

ViewerAlex: Found this through a reddit thread about Acacia Springs. When's the actual exploration start??

Carter grinned. "We haven't even promoted this yet. Chat, if you can hear me—" He waved at the camera. "Welcome. You're early and we love you for it."

"Carter, the test isn't miked yet," Evan said. "They can't hear you."

"They can see me wave. It's called engagement."

Derek got the harness sorted and straightened up, checking his reflection in a dead monitor. He adjusted the strap across his chest, then adjusted it again. "How do I look?"

"Like a guy who's about to enter an abandoned factory," Ava said from the floor, where she'd set up a small monitor of her own. She was replaying test footage; the brief clip they'd shot earlier as a camera check, just the interior of the garage from different angles.

"That's what I'm going for," Derek said.

On the main monitor, the chat updated.

> **CandyMan_1927:** *The blueprint is missing the eastern sublevel.*

Carter read it twice. Then he laughed. "Oh, we've got a superfan already. Someone's done their homework." He pointed at the screen. "CandyMan underscore 1927. Pre-stream superfan. Love it. Engage with them, Maddie. This is exactly the kind of viewer we want."

Maddie leaned toward the chat. Her mouth opened. Closed. She read the message again.

"Carter. The whiteboard isn't in the camera frame."

"What?"

"Camera two." She pointed. "Wide shot. The whiteboard is out of frame on the left. I checked the framing twenty minutes ago; it cuts off at the equipment stack. The blueprint isn't visible in the feed."

Carter looked at camera two's output. She was right. The wide shot captured the center of the garage with Derek, the gear and the lighting rigs. The whiteboard with its three-color blueprint sat a good four feet outside the frame edge.

"So they know the building," Carter said. "It's public record. The architectural plans are—"

"The eastern sublevel isn't in public records," Maddie said. "I found it in a county surveyor's addendum that was misfiled under residential permits. It took me two weeks to—" She stopped. Pushed her glasses up. "That sublevel isn't in any accessible record. I only found it because the surveyor numbered his pages wrong."

Evan had stopped typing.

The chat updated again.

*CandyMan_1963: Correction noted. Records
updated. Welcome to the preliminary assessment.*

The username had changed. Carter blinked at it. 1927 was gone. Now it read 1963.

"The dates," Maddie said quietly, almost to herself. "1927 is when the factory opened. 1963 is when it closed."

Nobody picked it up. Derek was checking his harness again. Carter was already reframing.

"Okay, that's a *committed* fan account," he said. "Somebody's running an ARG. Alternate reality game," he added for Derek's benefit. "This is incredible for engagement. Evan, are you seeing the viewer count?"

Evan's expression said he wished he wasn't. The number in the corner of the test stream had been seven. Now it read nineteen. Now twenty-three.

"Climbing," Evan confirmed. His voice was careful. Measured. "Test session on a private link shouldn't be indexing to public search. I haven't pushed any metadata yet." He paused. Typed something. Typed something else. "Which is fine."

"It's better than fine," Carter said. "It's working." He clapped his hands once, the sound sharp in the concrete space. "Everybody feel that? This is what momentum feels like."

On the floor behind him, Ava replayed the test footage one more time. Carter caught it in his peripheral vision: the slight hitch in her shoulders, the way she leaned closer to the small monitor until its blue light filled her eyes. She played the clip frame by frame. He could see her finger tapping the arrow key.

She stopped.

Her head tilted in that angle that meant she was seeing something the rest of them weren't. Her lips parted. She stared at the frozen frame for three full seconds, and Carter watched something move behind her expression.

Then she turned the monitor off and set it face-down on the concrete.

"Ava? Everything good with the test footage?"

"Hmm?" She looked up. Those dark eyes, slightly too wide. "Yeah. Fine. Just checking white balance."

Carter almost pressed it. He could see the question sitting right there, waiting: *What did you see?* But Ava's face had already rearranged itself into something neutral, and he had viewer counts to think about, and the chat was—

"Okay. Wild question." Derek's voice came from across the garage, and it had a strange quality to it. Baffled, almost embarrassed. He was standing completely still with one hand on his bodycam harness and the other hovering near his mouth. "Does anyone else taste... fruit candies right now? Just me?"

The room paused.

Carter's tongue pressed against the roof of his mouth. There it was; faint, source-less and unmistakable. Sugar. brighter than the burnt-coffee sweetness from the diner. Artificial, like someone had held an open bag of candy under his nose for half a second and pulled it away.

Riley's hand went to her wrist.

The taste was already gone.

"Probably the gear off-gassing," Evan said, but he was looking at his signal readout, not at Derek. "New electronics. Chemical coatings."

"That tasted nothing like a chemical coating," Derek said.

"I said *probably*."

The viewer count on the test stream read forty-one.

Carter swept the garage one more time, cataloging: gear packed, batteries charged, cameras tested. He pulled out his phone and hit record for a little video diary moment, just him and the lens. "Alright. Pre-stream test complete, signal's strong, and we've already got viewers finding us before we've even promoted. Chat's active. Energy's right." He grinned. Performing confidence came easy when the numbers were climbing. "Tonight, we go to the factory. Tonight, we go live."

He panned the phone in a slow arc across the garage. Equipment cases, the light stands. The whiteboard with the factory blueprint, still annotated in Maddie's handwriting with the eastern sublevel circled in red.

He ended the recording and pocketed the phone without reviewing it.

***

The gravel was wrong.

Carter noticed it the second his boot hit the lot. The surface gave too much, sinking a quarter-inch like packed earth that had been recently disturbed. Not the solid crunch of decades-old industrial ground. He filed it somewhere behind the adrenaline and kept walking.

The Delightful Candy Co. rose against the low sky like something that had grown rather than been built. Massive. Mid-century brick the color of dried blood, darkened further by fifty years of weather and neglect. Two smokestacks punched upward, blacker than the clouds behind them. The perimeter fence was chain-link and rust, the warning signs bleached by sun and rain until the text was more of a memory. AUTHORIZED PERSONNEL ONLY. TRESPASSERS WILL BE — the rest was gone.

Carter's A-cam was already rolling. The building was a perfect establishing shot.

"What is up, Explorers! Carter here, coming at you live from the gates of the Delightful Candy Company." He swept the camera in a slow arc, brick to smokestack to fence line, pitching his voice to be confident, conspiratorial, intimate. Like he was letting a hundred thousand people in on a secret, even though the viewer count had just crested ninety. "Abandoned since 1963. The heart of Acacia Springs, and the site of one of the most documented industrial disappearances in American history. Tonight, we're going inside. Tonight, you're coming with us."

The word *live* hung in the air a beat too long.

Behind him, Evan had the signal meter out. Carter could hear the faint clicking as he cycled through frequencies. "Okay, so — signal's structured," Evan said, half to Carter, half to his equipment. "I'm getting consistent handshake patterns I didn't set up. Like there's already network architecture here." He paused. "Which is fine."

"How's chat looking?" Carter called back.

Maddie had the tablet out, tilted against her hip. "First real wave coming in. Hundred and twelve. Hundred and twenty. They found us fast." She was scrolling, but her attention kept pulling away from the chat toward something else on the screen.

"Derek, you ready to make an entrance?"

Derek was already at the main door. Corrugated steel, industrial-gauge, the factory logo stamped dead center: a stylized candy wrapper with a smiling face that decades of oxidation had eroded into something leering. One eye had rusted through completely, leaving a dark socket. The mouth's upward curve had warped.

"Born ready," Derek said. His hands were in his jacket pockets. The night was mild, in the low sixties with barely a breeze.

To Carter's left, Ava stood motionless with a napkin pressed against the hood of the van, sketching with fast short strokes. She'd filled two on the drive over. Now a third. She wasn't looking at the building while she drew it.

"Ava, we need you on frame."

"One second." She didn't look up. Her pen stopped. Started again in a different spot. Stopped. "This building... Actually, never mind. One second."

Carter let it go. He swung the camera toward Riley.

She was ten feet from the door and not moving. Not performing hesitation — Carter had seen her perform for the camera, and this wasn't it. She was standing very still with her weight slightly back, like the ground itself was doing something she didn't trust. Her left hand pressed against her wrist. Not the casual trace he'd seen at the diner; pressing hard.

"Riles. You good?"

"Yeah." The word came out flat. Her eyes were on the building. Specifically on a window. High, upper right, third floor. "Yeah, I'm good."

Carter followed her gaze. The window held a faint amber glow. Warm without a source. It hadn't been there when they'd pulled in; he was certain of that because he'd scanned the building's silhouette from the road for exactly this kind of detail. No light then.

He chose not to think about it and turned the camera around instead.

Every phone in the group buzzed simultaneously.

Carter pulled his from his pocket. A notification: trending topic alert.

#SweetSilence

"Someone's doing our marketing for us," Carter said, grinning. He held the screen up toward the camera. "Chat, did one of you start this? Hashtag SweetSilence is trending."

He didn't check when it had started trending. He was already pivoting, already framing.

"Perfect," he muttered. "Cut to reaction... hold on this..."

"Carter." Maddie's voice. The quiet that meant she'd found a pattern. "Come look at this."

He crossed to her. The tablet showed a grid of photos; exterior shots of the factory taken by different people across different years. Forum posts, image uploads, a couple from an old online blog. Different cameras, different seasons, different times of day.

"What am I looking at?"

"Upper right window," Maddie said. "Every photo."

He looked. In the first image, daylight, a figure; dark and indistinct, but shaped like a person standing just behind the glass. In the second, dusk, same window and same shape. Third photo, fourth, seventh. All of them with the same window, same figure. Same position.

"Could be pareidolia," Carter said. "Pattern recognition in shadows."

"It could," Maddie agreed. She didn't sound like she agreed. She turned the tablet toward Derek.

Derek looked at the screen, then at the building. Then at the window on the third floor.

The glow flickered very slightly, and held.

"Yeah, that's a light," Derek said. "In a building with no power since 1963."

From somewhere inside — deep, muffled by brick and steel and distance — a sound. Rhythmic and metallic. The steady clank of machinery in motion.

They all heard it. The gravel-shuffle of six people going still at the same time.

"Tell me one of you planted a speaker in there," Derek said.

Nobody had.

Evan already had his meter up. He stood motionless for ten seconds, reading, then lowered it slowly. "Forty-seven BPM," he said. "Consistent. Mechanical." He put the meter away without further comment.

Carter was about to ask what that number meant when movement caught the edge of his vision. Loading dock, left side of the building, twenty yards out. A figure, standing in the shadow of the dock's concrete overhang.

"Hey!" Carter turned, camera tracking. "Hey! Excuse me —"

The figure stepped half into the lot's ambient light. Wrong clothes. Not wrong for the weather exactly, but wrong for *now*: high-waisted trousers, a collared shirt with the sleeves rolled in a way that looked period-specific. The kind of outfit Carter had seen in the factory's archived employee photos.

"You the film crew?" the figure called. Voice flat and conversational. Like they'd been waiting.

"We're a livestream," Carter called back, already moving toward them. "Are you, do you work for the property management? We have permission from the county to —"

He rounded the edge of the loading dock. Empty. The concrete platform, the rusted bay doors, the weeds pushing through expansion joints. There was no figure, no sound of retreating footsteps. No cover within thirty feet in any direction they could have reached in the two seconds Carter's eyes had been off them.

He stood there for a moment, camera still recording, and felt something cold settle into the space between his lungs.

Trespasser, he told himself. *Curious local. Moved faster than you thought.*

He walked back to the group. "Nobody there. Probably a local checking us out."

The chat had opinions.

> **ShadowWatcher99:** *that person's clothes are wrong. too wrong.*

> **NightOwl_Explores:** *they were asking about a FILM crew. who films here?*

> **CandyMan_1963:** *Welcome back. All crews*

accounted for.

Nobody on the team read the chat. They were all looking at the door.

Carter positioned himself beside Derek, camera angled to catch the group and the entrance in a single frame. Viewer count: a hundred and eighty-seven and climbing. He could feel the momentum like weather pressure.

"Alright," he said. "This is it. The Delightful Candy Company. Closed in 1963 under circumstances that have never been fully explained. Tonight we go inside, we go live, and we find out what this place has been hiding for sixty years."

Good. Clean. The kind of line that opened a trailer.

Riley was beside the door now. Carter hadn't seen her move. She stood with one hand trailing against the corrugated steel, and her face had that expression that was older than twenty-three.

"My great-grandfather used to call it the sweet silence," she said. Quiet and almost to herself, except the bodycam mic would catch it perfectly. "The moment right before the machines stopped." A beat. "He meant it as a warning."

Carter felt the hairs on his arms lift. He also felt the shot.

"Perfect title," he said.

Riley looked at him. Something was in her eyes that wasn't quite contempt and wasn't quite pity, like she'd known he would say exactly that and had decided to let it happen.

Derek gripped the cold metal of the door handle. Carter could see his fingers tighten, adjust and tighten again.

"On three, yeah?"

Nobody counted and Derek pulled. The handle resisted, then gave with a shriek of corroded metal that made Maddie flinch and sent a scatter of rust flakes drifting down like orange snow.

Warm air hit them; almost body-temperature, rolling out through the widening gap like an exhalation. And riding on it an artificial sweetness so thick Carter could taste it on his teeth. Sugar and machine oil and something underneath both. It felt organic and patient, like fruit left to ripen in a sealed room for decades past the point of sweetness.

The viewer count hit two hundred. The window on the third floor brightened, just slightly, in the same heartbeat.

Riley stepped through first.

She didn't pause, didn't announce it. One moment she was beside the door and the next she was past the threshold, her silhouette swallowed by the interior dark. She didn't look back.

Carter read it as courage. Behind him, Ava's pen stopped on the napkin. She watched Riley disappear inside and her expression said something else entirely.

One by one they followed. Derek. Maddie, tablet clutched to her chest. Ava, tucking the napkin into her jacket. Evan, eyes on the signal meter, walking blind.

Carter went last. He paused in the doorway for a single held breath, camera up and framing the interior dark. The stream was live and climbing. He stepped through.

The door swung shut behind him with a clang that traveled through the floor and up the walls and into spaces above them they couldn't see. The echo deepened, lengthened. It resolved into something rhythmic that might have been the machinery sound from outside or might have been the building settling around them like a jaw.

The stream was live with two hundred and fourteen viewers. Two hundred and nineteen.

Above the loading dock outside, a security camera hung from a rusted bracket. Analog and decades old. Its housing was angled toward the wall, pointed at nothing and capturing nothing. The small red light on its underside was on. In the footage it recorded, feeding to an archive no one was monitoring, the group was visible crossing the lot and entering the building.

The timestamp on the feed read: **1963.**

2

The flashlight beams didn't reach the ceiling.

Maddie registered this as data before she registered it as fear. She swept her light upward and the beam dissolved into dark somewhere above thirty feet without catching steel or concrete or anything at all. The production floor of the Delightful Candy Company had been documented in the county surveyor's report as having twenty-two-foot clearances. She'd memorized that number. She'd memorized all the numbers.

The ceiling was not twenty-two feet above them.

"Based on the blueprints, this main floor should be approximately —" She caught herself. Nobody needed the lecture right now. She pulled her tablet up and started cross-referencing.

The tablet's battery read one hundred percent.

She'd checked it in the van. Seventy-three; she hadn't plugged it in. She stared at the number for two full seconds, then swiped past it and opened her floor plan overlay. Later, save it for later.

Around her, the group's flashlights and phone screens carved the dark into overlapping wedges that seemed to compress the space between them while leaving everything beyond their perimeter thick and absolute. The production floor stretched in every direction: long rows of silent machinery, conveyor belts frozen mid-run, wrapping arms locked in the act of reaching. Mixing vats the size of small cars. Roller assemblies trailing candy wrappers that crunched underfoot with every step, a brittle sound like walking through a field of dead leaves.

"This is incredible," Carter breathed. He was panning his A-cam in a slow sweep, and even through his performer's voice Maddie could hear something underneath. "Chat, are you seeing this? Original equipment, untouched since 1963. This is a time capsule."

Maddie moved through a cold patch; sudden, localized, like stepping through a doorway into a walk-in freezer. And then out the other side into air that was nearly warm. No ductwork above, no vents she could identify. She logged it on her tablet:

> *Temperature anomaly, grid position C-4, duration*
> *approx. 2 seconds, no apparent source.*

"Stay tight, everyone," Riley said from somewhere to Maddie's left. Her voice was controlled and level in that way Maddie had learned meant the opposite of calm. "We don't know this floor plan yet."

"I do," Maddie said automatically, then corrected: "I have the surveyed floor plan. Though the dimensions aren't matching what I'm seeing. This room is larger than documented. By a significant margin."

"How significant?" Evan asked. He was six feet away, staring at his signal meter like it owed him money.

"I'll know when I finish mapping, but the western wall should be visible from here. It isn't."

No one responded to that. The candy wrappers crinkled under their feet.

Derek was walking a half-step behind her and slightly to her right. Close enough that she could feel the displacement of air when he moved, which was fine. Normal positioning. His flashlight swept the machinery rows in methodical arcs, left to right, pausing on each piece of equipment before moving to the next.

He stopped.

"Did that —"

Maddie turned. Derek was facing Line 3 : the original 1927 installation, she knew immediately, the mechanical wrapping arms with the distinctive pivot joints. His beam was locked on one of the wrapping arms, frozen mid-rotation in a position that should have been mechanically impossible without counterweight adjustment.

"Did what?" she asked.

Derek's jaw worked. His flashlight didn't waver. Three seconds. Five.

"Never mind. Probably just our lights playing with the shadows."

Maddie looked at him. He didn't look back. His hand went to his pocket — the coin, she knew — and came out empty. He kept walking.

She turned back to her tablet and almost walked into a cluster of candy wrappers near the east entrance. They were piled in a loose arrangement on the floor, curled edges catching her light in a pattern that…

She stopped and tilted her head. The wrappers were arranged in concentric arcs radiating from a central point, and the negative space between them formed a shape she recognized from somewhere specific and immediate. Riley's tattoo. The candy wrapper design on Riley's wrist.

Maddie raised her tablet and took a screenshot. When she looked back at the floor, the wrappers were scattered randomly. Just litter and decades of neglect.

She stared for a long moment, then typed into her notes:

> *Wrapper arrangement near east entrance: possible pareidolia. Document and revisit.*

Her fingers were shaking slightly and she attributed it to the cold patches.

"Guys." Carter's voice had that hook in it. The pitch-voice. "Check the viewer count."

Maddie crossed to him. His phone showed the stream dashboard with four hundred and ninety-three viewers. As she watched, the number blinked and reset to baseline. Then it climbed, fast and smooth, like a counter on a timer: five hundred. Eight hundred. Twelve hundred. It passed fifteen hundred without slowing and locked at one thousand, nine hundred and sixty-three.

And held.

"Those aren't random numbers," Maddie said. The connection was already forming. "493 is the recorded headcount for the final production shift. 1,963 is the year —"

> *StreamFan23: wait how did i even get here?? this autoplayed after a video i never watch*
>
> *ViewerAlex: same — it showed up in my recommended and i don't follow any urbex channels at all*
>
> *NightOwl_Explores: it tagged three of my friends who have never watched anything like this. none of us clicked it. it just opened.*
>
> *TechieTom: i'm seeing this stream promoted on pages it has no algorithmic reason to appear on. the tag categories don't match the content. something external is pushing the distribution.*
>
> *CandyMan_1963: Welcome. We're glad you found us.*

"This place is *delivering*, people." Carter pumped his fist, already turning to the camera with his grin back in place. "Chat, you seeing these numbers? We haven't even left the main floor and we're pushing two thousand viewers. This is what happens when a location is real."

Maddie stared at him; he'd already moved on. She hadn't.

On Evan's secondary monitor which was propped on a cable case, still recording the chat feed, messages were scrolling:

> *TechieTom: those numbers are sequential dates. 1927 open, 1963 close, 493 = the number of employees on the final day shift. how is this platform surfacing that data.*
>
> *CandyMan_1963: All counts are accurate.*
>
> *TechieTom: side note — CandyMan_1963 has been in this chat since before the stream went public. account creation timestamp predates the channel's existence by three years. that's not possible for a normal viewer account.*
>
> *TechieTom: probably nothing. logging it.*

The monitor was angled slightly away from the group. Nobody read it. Evan was fifteen feet away, running diagnostics on his primary rig with his back turned.

"Okay, here's what I'm thinking." Carter clapped his hands. The sound was swallowed by the space almost before it reached them. "We need to cover ground. Main floor, the catwalks, and the administrative wing. That's three zones and six of us. Maddie, you've been talking about the admin records since day one. That's your priority. Derek, big guy, smart girl, good combo. Take the east corridor."

Maddie felt Derek shift beside her. The reduction landed the way Carter's reductions always did: accurate enough to be dismissive, casual enough to be plausible.

"Applied percussive maintenance," Derek said lightly. "I kick doors open, she reads what's behind them."

He said it to the camera. He said it for her.

"Riley, Ava, you're with me on the main floor and catwalks. Evan holds base camp here, keeps the stream architecture running. Ten-minute check-ins on comms."

"Carter." Riley's voice was flat. "We should stay together."

"We've got six cameras, four comms units, and a building that isn't going to explore itself. This is standard protocol, Riles."

"Standard protocol for what? We've been inside for four minutes."

"Standard for making the best stream we've ever produced." Carter met her eyes. Whatever he saw there, he didn't flinch from. "Ten-minute check-ins. Anything feels wrong, we regroup. But right now the building's giving us everything and we need to be in position to catch it."

Riley's hand was on her wrist, pressing. Maddie could see the tension in her fingers from six feet away.

"Fine," Riley said. "Ten minutes."

Ava hadn't spoken. She was standing at the edge of the group's light, her sketchpad open, her pen moving in quick strokes that Maddie couldn't track. She was drawing something. Not the room; Maddie could tell because Ava's eyes weren't on the room. They were on the upper catwalks, fixed on a point in the darkness above Line 3. Her pen was filling half a page with a shape that had too many angles for anything architectural.

"Ava?" Maddie asked.

Ava blinked. Looked down at her page. Closed the sketchpad.

"Coming," she said. "Just... getting the texture."

The group split. Maddie and Derek moved east, their flashlights cutting parallel beams through dust that rose around them in slow spirals. Neither of them had disturbed it. The wrappers crunched underfoot, and underneath that sound — far underneath — Maddie thought she heard the faintest tick of metal on metal, rhythmic and patient, like a clock that had forgotten how to stop.

The comms crackled once. Carter's voice, already more distant than the distance explained: "Ten-minute check-in. Go."

Behind them, on Evan's secondary monitor, still recording with nobody watching, the chat count climbed. And climbed.

***

The filing cabinet drawer came out smoothly for something that should have been rusted shut for sixty years.

Maddie caught it with both hands and set it on the nearest desk, already scanning the tab dividers. Personnel records, A through D. Alphabetized, intact, the paper yellowed but legible. She felt the specific, private thrill that came with primary sources, the same feeling she got in university archives when the librarian brought out the boxes nobody had requested in decades.

"This is organized," she said, half to Derek, half to the tablet's voice memo. "Somebody maintained these files. The indexing system is consistent through at least — " She flipped through tabs. "Through at least 1962. Final entries look like October '63."

"Great." Derek was not looking at the files. Derek was looking at the lantern.

It sat on a desk at the far end of the corridor, forty feet from the collapsed section of drop ceiling where they'd entered the administrative wing. A camping lantern: LED, compact, the kind you'd buy for maybe thirty dollars. Its light was clean and white and entirely wrong for this building. Everything else in the admin wing existed in a palette of rust and water damage and nicotine-colored decay. The lantern looked like it had been placed there an hour ago.

"Someone's been in here," Derek said.

"Someone's been in here *recently*," Maddie corrected. She reached for the next drawer. "Urban explorers, probably. The county permit office said there's been consistent trespassing since —"

A sound from the office beyond the lantern. Not mechanical, human. Someone clearing their throat.

Derek's flashlight snapped toward it. His body shifted a half-step forward, angling himself between the sound and Maddie, automatic as breathing. His free hand went to his pocket.

"Hello?" Derek called.

A figure stepped into the lantern's glow from the adjacent doorway, and Maddie's first thought was *costume*. Flannel shirt over a band t-shirt she didn't recognize, baggy jeans cuffed at the ankle, a backward baseball cap. He was holding a camcorder; bulky, boxy, the kind with a flip-out viewfinder. And he was already filming them.

> ***FilmNerd_404:*** *wait is that a JVC GR-AX series? that's a mid-90s consumer camcorder. that's not a prop. someone's actually been shooting on tape in there.*

"Oh thank god." His voice was quick, relieved, pitched with a kind of gladness that seemed too large for the situation. "Have you seen a group: three people, Steadicam and a sound rig? They went around that corner like twenty minutes ago and I haven't —"

He stopped. His camcorder dipped. He was looking at Derek's flashlight; the tactical LED, twelve hundred lumens, brushed aluminum body.

"Where did you get that?"

Derek looked at his flashlight. Looked at the guy. "Online?"

"Right. Yeah." The guy blinked. Recovered. "Sorry, I just… it's really bright. I'm Thomas. Thomas Martinez. I'm a film student; we're doing a documentary about local legends, and my crew came through here but I lost them in the east stairwell." He gestured vaguely behind him with the camcorder. "You guys are exploring too?"

> **FilmNerd_404:** *okay i'm sorry but that camera is genuinely cool. thomas right? what are you documenting?*

"We're livestreaming," Maddie said. She'd already categorized him: fellow documentarian, indie production, vintage equipment enthusiast. The camcorder made sense in that framework. Analog revival was everywhere right now. "I'm Maddie. This is Derek. We're doing a live exploration for our channel."

"Livestreaming?" Thomas said.

He said it the way someone says a word they recognize from print but have never heard used as a verb.

"Like, broadcasting live," Maddie clarified. "To an audience. In real time."

"No, I know what… yeah." Thomas nodded, fast. "Cool. That's cool. How many people watching?"

"Almost two thousand, last count."

His eyebrows went up. Genuinely impressed. "On what network?"

Network. An odd word choice. Maddie noted it and moved on. "Platform. It's a streaming platform. Are you doing documentation work too? Because these files —" She turned back to the cabinet, pulling the drawer toward the lantern's light. "These are the original personnel records. If you're making a documentary about the factory, this is primary source material."

Thomas was at her shoulder in three steps, camcorder still running. The eagerness in his movement was the specific eagerness of someone who cared about archives. Maddie recognized it because she owned it.

"No way. Are those alphabetized? The county records office told us everything was destroyed in the closure."

"Clearly not. Look at the indexing; someone maintained a cross-reference system." She pulled a file at random. Henderson, Patricia. Hired 1951. Quality Control Division. The photograph stapled to the inner cover showed a woman in her thirties, hair pinned under a factory cap, expression carefully neutral. "Employee photos, hire dates, department assignments. This is —"

"This is the motherload," Thomas finished. He was grinning. "Oh man, if I can get this on camera. The light's terrible in here but I've got a —" He reached into his jacket and produced a small clip-on light, incandescent and warm. "There. Okay, can you hold that file open? Just like that?"

They fell into it. The rhythm of two people who understood documentation finding each other in an unlikely place. Thomas asked about her research methodology and she found herself explaining her cross-referencing system. The blueprint overlays, the archived newspaper clippings, the county surveyor's data. All with a fluency she rarely achieved in conversation. He listened actively, with follow-up questions that showed he'd actually processed what she said.

"You're thorough," he said. "Most people who come to places like this just want the jump scare. The B-roll. You actually want to understand the system."

"The system is the story," Maddie said. "The building is just the container."

"Yeah." Thomas's smile had something wistful in it. "Yeah, that's exactly… my advisor keeps saying the same thing. Document the structure, not the spectacle."

Derek stood three feet back, watching. He'd relaxed enough to lean against a desk, but his flashlight was still in his hand and his eyes hadn't left Thomas. Friendly on the surface. Counting exits underneath.

Maddie's hand brushed one of the papers affixed to the wall near the filing cabinet. She paused. The texture under her fingers was wrong; not quite sticky, not quite dry. Like something had been applied as an adhesive and then fossilized in an intermediate state. Sweet-smelling, faintly. She pulled her hand back and wiped it on her jeans without thinking.

"What's holding these up?" she asked.

Thomas glanced at the papers. "Some kind of residue. Sugar-based, I think. It's all over the admin wing. On the walls, in the desk drawers. Like someone spilled syrup and it just... set."

He said it like he'd had time to notice. Like he'd been here long enough to develop a theory.

"Thomas, how long have you been in the building?" Maddie asked.

"Oh, not long. Maybe…" He checked his watch. Digital display, chunky plastic case. "Like forty-five minutes? My crew came in through the loading dock and we split up to cover more ground, which in hindsight was—" He laughed. "Not the best plan. I'm sure they're around here somewhere."

Maddie looked at the lantern. LED camping lantern, standard battery. If he'd been here forty-five minutes, the battery was fine. If he'd been here much longer than that, with the settled quality of the space around him, his comfort with the layout. The way he'd moved through the adjoining offices like someone navigating a familiar apartment; the battery should have been dead.

She didn't complete the thought. Thomas was already pointing at her tablet.

"Can I see the blueprint? I've been trying to find the records room. The main one, not these satellite offices. There should be a central archive somewhere on this floor."

"Based on the surveyor's report, it's at the intersection of the B and C corridors." Maddie pulled up the overlay and handed him the tablet. "Here, the highlighted section."

Thomas took it. The lock screen illuminated with the date and time:

November 15, 2024, 9:47 PM.

His face did something.

It was fast. A micro-expression that cascaded through surprise and confusion and something that looked almost like grief, before he smoothed it into neutral. Derek saw it. Maddie caught only the tail end, the recovery, which she read as him processing the blueprint data.

"Nice display," Thomas said. His voice was even. "The resolution on this is… what is this, like a Retina screen?"

"It's a standard tablet."

"Right." He handed it back. His fingers lingered on the edge for a half-second longer than necessary, as if he didn't want to let it go.

Thomas looked at her tablet setup, the capture settings visible on the screen. He tilted his head at it. "How long have you been documenting?"

"This building, about three hours," Maddie said. "Urban exploration generally, four years."

"Right." He nodded, but he was looking at his own camcorder, not hers. "I keep losing track of how long I've been on this one. I came in to document the local legend angle; haunted factory, good B-roll. My crew was with me." He turned the camcorder over in his hands, checking something on the casing. "And then they went around a corner and I kept filming. Because that's what you do, right? You keep the camera up. Even when things get—" He stopped. Chose a different word. "—strange. You keep the record." He glanced up at her. "I think I've been keeping the record longer than I planned."

Maddie processed this. *"How long is longer than you planned?"*

Thomas looked at his camcorder again. He found what he'd been checking on the casing: a sticker, worn at the edges. He touched the edge of it. "I keep meaning to check the tape counter. I just—" He didn't finish. He looked up with the quick, bright recovery of someone changing the subject. "What's your audio setup? Because the ambient sound in this wing is incredible."

Maddie let him change it. She pulled out her audio recorder.

Then, carefully, he asked: "What year is it right now? On that thing?" He gestured at the tablet.

Maddie looked at him. Looked at Derek. Derek had straightened off the desk.

"...2024," she said.

Thomas stood very still. The camcorder in his other hand she noticed now, the boxy compact VHS form factor that she'd seen in her parents' wedding video. It was pointed at the floor. Its red recording light was on.

"Right," he said. There was a long pause. Something moved behind his eyes like weather. "Right, yeah. Obviously."

He picked up the camcorder. His hands were not steady.

"The records room," he said, and his voice was almost normal. "I can take you there. I know where it is."

Behind them, on the stream that neither Maddie nor Derek was monitoring, the chat was moving fast:

> **RetroTech_Randy:** *that's a GR-AX something. those stopped being manufactured in 1999. that's not a prop, that's USED.*

> **HauntHunter_Sarah:** *His jacket. Look at his jacket. That is not thrift store vintage. that is actually vintage. Cross-referencing missing persons reports*

from Acacia Springs, 1990s.

CandyMan_1963: *The documentation team arrived on schedule.*

Thomas was already moving toward the corridor, his lantern in one hand and the camcorder in the other, navigating the collapsed ceiling tiles and fallen acoustic panels with the sureness of someone who'd walked this path many times. Derek fell into step behind him. Maddie followed, her tablet back in her bag, her fingers still faintly sticky with whatever substance held those papers to the wall.

One of those papers, partially visible behind a filing cabinet Derek had brushed past, had handwriting on it. Handwritten in a loose, youthful scrawl.

The date in the corner was 1997.

Derek saw it. His step hitched, just barely. He kept walking.

On the stream, the viewer count ticked up each time the camera caught a frame of Thomas's VHS recorder. The number climbed in small, patient increments, like something keeping count.

***

The records room was circular, which made no sense for an administrative space.

Maddie registered this as she crossed the threshold. Filing cabinets were arranged in radiating rows from a central desk, floor to ceiling, like a processing hub designed for maximum retrieval efficiency. Thomas held his lantern up and the light caught metal drawer faces in every direction, hundreds of them, labeled and indexed with typed cards slotted into brass holders.

"This is it," Thomas said. He set the lantern on the central desk. "This is the archive."

Behind the lantern, something glowed.

A terminal. Cathode-ray monitor, the heavy glass kind, its casing the color of old bone. The screen was on. Amber text on black, a cursor blinking at the bottom of a data field with the patience of a heartbeat. No power cable ran to any visible outlet, no hum of a hard drive. Just the screen, steady and warm, casting Thomas's face in copper light.

Maddie went for the filing cabinets first. Morgan. She needed Morgan.

The M-section was in the fourth row, third cabinet from the floor. She pulled the drawer and it slid open on oiled tracks, silent, the files inside arranged with the precision of a living office. No water damage and no rodent chewing. No foxing on the paper. She flipped through tabs: Mercer, Mitchell, Monroe, and found it.

Morgan, Robert J. Quality Control Supervisor. Hired: March 1961.

She pulled the file. The paper inside was pristine. Not preserved-in-a-museum pristine. It felt wrong between her fingers, too smooth, the fibers unnaturally intact. Employee photograph: a tall man, rigid posture with horn-rimmed glasses, the "Quality Control" patch on his lab coat rendered in sharp detail. His expression was careful and watchful.

She flipped to the final page. A single typed note beneath the last performance review:

Incident: Unresolved. Investigation: Suspended. Status: Processing.

Processing. Not "processed." Not "terminated." Not any of the usual euphemisms for a closed file. Present tense; ongoing.

"These records are complete," Maddie said. Her voice was steady. She was aware of it being steady because she was making it steady. "Everything is here. This should not be possible."

She snapped a picture of the file, both sides of every page. Her hands worked automatically.

Behind her, Thomas stood at the terminal.

He'd been standing there since they entered, she realized. His body was angled slightly forward, his camcorder lowered and forgotten, and the amber light turned the lenses of his eyes into small flat discs. He was reading something on the screen with an expression she could identify with clinical precision. The micro-tension around the orbicularis oculi, the slight parting of the lips, the complete stillness of someone receiving a diagnosis.

She moved toward him. He shifted his body. Subtle, a half-turn that put his shoulder between her and the screen.

Too late.

The screen showed an employee directory. Active. Scrollable. The cursor blinked beside an entry:

> *Martinez, Thomas A. — Documentation Division*
>
> *Entry Date: October 12, 1997*
>
> *Status: Processing — Ongoing*

"Don't—" Thomas started. Stopped. Swallowed. "It's just. The screen is bright from this angle."

Maddie looked at his face. He looked at hers. Something passed between them that was not a conversation and did not need to be.

She went back to the filing cabinets.

On the wall behind the terminal, a factory floor map covered an eight-by-six-foot section. The full complex layout: production lines, loading docks, administrative wing, east wing, boiler room. It had been annotated. Three different handwritings. Two ink types, one blue-black and crisp, one faded brown that predated it by decades. The most recent annotations with directional arrows, circled junctions, a route traced in red. They were in a loose, youthful scrawl.

Thomas's handwriting. Mapping routes through a building he'd said he'd been in for forty-five minutes.

Maddie pulled out her tablet to capture the map and the screen lit with notifications. The stream chat, still running, populated her display in a cascade of messages she hadn't been monitoring. Most of it was noise. One was pinned.

> ***HauntHunter_Sarah:*** *I found him. Thomas Martinez. Film student, 22, went missing from the Delightful Candy Co. location October 1997. Declared dead 2001. There's a newspaper article. I'm linking it now.*

Maddie read it.

She looked up at Thomas, who was standing at the terminal with both hands flat on the desk, reading something on the amber screen with a face that was very carefully not reacting.

She closed her tablet.

Derek was at the doorway, holding the comms tablet as a secondary monitor. His eyes moved across the screen, stopped, and moved across it again. Reading something twice. His jaw set in a way that Maddie had learned meant he was performing calm rather than experiencing it.

"Speed up," he said. His voice was easy, conversational. "We should grab what we need and get back to base camp."

From somewhere beneath them a sound began. Low and rhythmic, felt in the sternum before the ears processed it. Metal engaging metal in sequence, the cascading ignition of systems designed to operate in concert. Purposeful.

Thomas heard it first. His head turned toward the floor, then toward the east wall, then a point in space that corresponded to nothing visible. His face changed in a way Maddie couldn't categorize.

"That's machinery," Derek said. Flat, factual. He let it sit for a beat. "That's active machinery."

On the stream, in a chat that none of them were watching:

> **RetroTech_Randy:** *production line audio signature detected. that's startup sequencing.*

> **CandyMan_1963:** *Final quality review: scheduled.*

Thomas stepped away from the terminal. He picked up his lantern. His camcorder was recording and he held it like a talisman, pointed at nothing, the red light steady.

"Left here, then through the door at the end," he said. His voice was almost normal. "I know the way out."

They moved. Thomas led, navigating without consulting the map he'd already annotated, past filing cabinets and through a connecting passage that didn't appear on Maddie's blueprint overlay. Derek stayed at the rear, his flashlight sweeping behind them in controlled arcs. The production sounds built beneath their feet: a pulse, a rhythm, like the factory was remembering how to breathe.

In the corridor, Thomas slowed at a junction. To the left: the route back to the administrative wing and base camp. To the right: a passage that curved downward toward the production floor. He looked right. Held the look for two seconds. Three.

Then he turned left.

Maddie's comms crackled. Carter's voice, too loud in the quiet: "Check-in. What've you got?"

She opened her mouth. She had the Morgan file photographed, the terminal record seen, HauntHunter_Sarah's message unacknowledged, and Thomas Martinez walking next to her with a camcorder that hadn't been manufactured in twenty-five years.

"We found something," she said. "And someone."

3

The sketchpad app had three saved images Ava hadn't drawn.

She noticed while Riley was pulling her kit together in the corridor outside the records room, while Thomas stood six feet away pretending to check his camcorder's battery with hands that were steadier than his breathing. The transition had been wordless: Maddie and Derek darted past them toward base camp with the Morgan file and a comms check-in schedule, leaving Ava and Riley to push forward into the quality control wing. Thomas had simply come with them. Nobody had discussed it. Nobody had asked him not to.

Ava opened the app to sketch the first testing station they passed and the gallery thumbnail showed three entries. Timestamped. The first at 2:14 AM, six hours before they'd entered the factory. The second at 3:47. The third at 5:02. She'd been asleep for all of them.

They showed interior spaces. Glass partitions, testing instruments on metal counters. A long, low-ceilinged corridor that she was currently standing in.

She stopped walking.

"You okay?" Riley was three steps ahead, her flashlight sweeping the row of stations that stretched before them. The quality control section was exactly as wrong as the app had rendered it. Fluorescent tubes overhead, half dead, the working ones blinking slowly at irregular intervals. Like something measuring them.

"Yeah. Just… the app's being weird." Ava swiped through the images. The detail was extraordinary; she could see the clipboards on their hooks, the half-filled forms, the glass partitions reflecting light sources that didn't exist in the drawings. The third image showed a shadow that fell across testing station four without any object to cast it.

She turned the tablet toward Thomas. He looked at the images. Looked at the room. His camcorder came up and he filmed the app screen in silence, holding the shot for five full seconds before lowering it.

He said nothing. That was worse.

"Thomas?"

"Good resolution on that app," he said. His voice was the careful neutral of someone choosing words like steps across ice. "What software is that?"

"Procreate."

"Cool." He walked ahead. The camcorder stayed up.

The quality control section smelled different from the corridors they'd come through. Chemical and sweet in equal measure, but *cleaner*. Antiseptic almost, like a laboratory that happened to process sugar. The floor was the strangest part. Swept, the grit arranged in curves that, if Ava tilted her head at the right angle, looked intentional. Compositional, like someone had used a push broom as a drawing tool.

She took a picture. She'd figure out what it meant later.

Riley was already at the far end, where a filing cabinet stood open. The top drawer extended, as though someone had pulled it out and walked away mid-task. Or as though someone had known they were coming.

"Riley, wait—"

But Riley's fingers were already in the files, and her body had gone very still in the way it went still when something connected. The tattoo on her wrist; the candy wrapper design, the tribute to the great-grandfather she'd never met. It was visible as she reached into the drawer, and Ava watched

Riley's other hand drift to it unconsciously. *Pressing* it, like it was warm. Like it was pulling.

"It was on top," Riley said quietly. She held a file. "It was just sitting right on top."

Ava moved toward her, stepping past testing station four. In her peripheral vision, the shadow at station four shifted. A settling, like a person adjusting their weight from one foot to the other. She kept her eyes forward.

"Okay, chat's flagging the shadow by station four," she said, reading the tablet's notification bar without looking up. "And… okay, several of you. I see it. Looking now."

She looked directly at it. The shadow was a shadow. Normal geometry. Fluorescent source overhead, instrument casting a predictable shape on the floor.

"Looks normal to me." She turned back to Riley. In her peripheral vision, behind her now, the shadow didn't look normal at all. "But I'm going to… yeah, I'm not going to look directly at it anymore."

Riley wasn't listening. She was reading.

"Quality Control Supervisor Robert Morgan. Performance: Exemplary. Commendations—" Her voice caught. Quieter: "They commended him. Right up until—"

She didn't finish. Her thumb moved across the page, tracing a line of text, and her expression did something complicated that Ava didn't interrupt.

On the tablet, the chat was moving fast.

> **HauntHunter_Sarah:** *emotional yield. that's not a candy quality metric. that's not anything to do with candy.*

> **TechieTom:** *cross-referencing. that terminology appears in declassified behavioral research documents. it's a measure of psychological response*

> *output. they were running psych experiments in a candy factory.*
>
> ***CandyMan_1963:*** *Quality standards were maintained at all times.*

Ava read the chat. She looked at Riley, who was still staring at the name, at the commendations, at the performance metrics that said her great-grandfather had been excellent at his job right up until the job became something else.

Riley hadn't read the column heading. *Emotional Yield: Subject Interaction.* The numbers beside Robert Morgan's name were high. Exceptional. Whatever they were measuring, he had produced a lot of it.

Ava photographed the document. She didn't read the column aloud.

"Chat's going a bit wild about that document, by the way," she said instead. Gentle, giving Riley the choice.

Riley closed the file, held it against her chest. Her wrist, the tattooed one, was pressed against the paper and Ava could see the faintest tremor in her fingers.

From beyond the far wall a low sound was building. Past the door at the corridor's end, the door that the factory map said led to the main production line. The same that they'd heard in the records room but closer now, more articulated.

Thomas had been standing slightly apart from them since they entered the section. He was near the door. Not close enough to touch it, but close enough that his camcorder was pointed at the gap beneath it, where the faintest light leaked through. The cool industrial white of overhead fixtures on a factory floor.

"We should probably not go through that door at the end," he said.

Riley looked up from the file. "Why?"

"It's more efficient to circle back." He pointed toward a branching corridor to the left, where a sign read TESTING LABORATORY — AUTHORIZED PERSONNEL. "That way connects to the east wing. I'd rather go around."

Derek's voice crackled on the comms clipped to Ava's bag: "Rather go around what?"

Thomas looked at the comms unit and something crossed his face. More people were listening, connected. An audience he couldn't see.

"The long way," he said, to the room rather than the comms. "Always better to take the long way."

He was already walking. Riley followed, the file still pressed to her chest. Ava lingered for two seconds. Long enough to see, through the testing laboratory's narrow window, that the equipment inside was on. Not standby. Actively cycling, instruments with lights that moved and read and measured. And at the central testing station, something that looked, from this distance and this angle and in this bad stuttering light, very much like a person.

ShadowWatcher99: there's someone in that room

CandyMan_1963: Quality assessment: proceeding on schedule.

***

The testing laboratory door was unlocked. The handle turned under Ava's palm with the smooth resistance of a mechanism recently oiled.

The room was clean.

That was the first wrong thing and the worst one. Every surface gleamed under overhead panels that shouldn't have been working but were, casting the even, shadowless light of a space designed for precision observation. Glass chambers lined the left wall, floor to ceiling, each one sealed and labeled with a typewritten card. Inside them: candy samples. Rows of them, in colors Ava's brain reached for and couldn't name.

Not the red of cherry or strawberry or any food that had ever existed. Something more *saturated,* that bypassed the color-processing part of her brain and landed somewhere in her chest. The next chamber held a shade that she could only describe as the feeling of being watched. The one after that was the color of a word you've forgotten.

She was an artist, she named colors for a living. These didn't have names.

"Chat, are you seeing this?" She held her tablet steady, panning across the chambers. "She's, yeah, okay. Zoom. Hold on."

At the central testing station, a woman was working.

Small with impeccable posture. Laboratory coat pressed and white except where stains spread across the hem in patterns that blinked faintly, darkening and lightening with a rhythm Ava could feel in her molars. Hair pulled back in a practical twist that moved, occasionally, in a direction that had nothing to do with air currents. A clipboard in her left hand, a pen in her right.

The pen moved down, across, up. Notation complete. Flip the page. Down, across, up. Identical notation. Flip the page.

"She's doing the same motion. She hasn't looked up."

The sound of pen on paper was metronomic. Perfectly regular. Ava counted without meaning to: forty-seven beats per minute. The same pulse Evan had measured at the factory entrance, the rhythm he'd called impossible because it matched no known mechanical cycle.

Riley had stopped in the doorway. Thomas was behind her and slightly to the left, positioned at the threshold the way you'd position yourself near an exit on a plane. His camcorder was up but pointed at the floor.

HistoryBuff_Marie: can you zoom into the clipboard? i'm reading "emotional resonance: 94th percentile" — what does that mean for candy

***TechieTom:** it's a psych research output. someone was running emotional extraction experiments here.*

***ShadowWatcher99:** she's been doing this same motion with the pen for like three minutes. the exact same motion.*

Ava zoomed in. The clipboard swam into focus through the tablet's camera: pages and pages beneath the current one, each covered in the same notation in the same hand. Not variations. Copies of the same quality assessment performed on the same samples, recorded in the same handwriting with the same results.

Emotional resonance: 94th percentile. Extraction viability: confirmed. Processing recommendation: proceed.

She read the chat responses aloud to Riley and Thomas. Behind her, she heard Thomas take a small step backward toward the door.

Riley moved forward.

"Riley—"

"Robert Morgan," Riley said. Not loudly. Almost to herself, the way you'd test a match against a striker. Gently, to see if it catches.

It caught.

The pen stopped mid-stroke, the way a video freezes on a bad connection. The woman at the testing station didn't look up but her body shifted. A stutter in the loop, like a record skipping, and for one fractured second she was present in the room with them. Her eyes moved and found Riley. The recognition in them was immediate and specific and terrible.

Then the machinery in the wall behind the testing station cycled. A low hum, mechanical and deliberate, the sound of something engaging. Clara's pen touched the paper. Down, across, up. Flip.

Gone.

> **CandyKid_98:** *she just reacted. she heard you.*

Riley's hand was on her wrist. The tattooed one. Ava could see it from where she stood. The candy wrapper design was visible at the edge of Riley's sleeve and beneath it, the skin was flushed. Not uniformly like a rash. The lines of the tattoo themselves were darker and more defined, as if the ink were being refreshed from underneath.

Riley didn't address it. The camera was on.

Then another message scrolled across Ava's tablet, and she read it before she thought about whether she should.

> **CandyKid_98:** *that's my great-great-grandmother.*
> *Clara Lee. she disappeared from this factory in 1963.*
> *we never found out what happened to her.*

Ava read it aloud. The words landed in the room like stones in still water. Silence.

The comms were open. They'd been open since the split.

From the admin wing, after a beat that was a little too long, Maddie's voice came through; quiet, with the particular flatness she used when she was controlling something:

"Say that name again."

Ava looked at the tablet. At the message. At Clara, who had not resumed her loop. "Clara Lee," she said.

The comms returned static. Then Derek's voice, lower: "Maddie." A pause. "We'll talk about it at check-in."

The comms went quiet.

Clara's pen paused. The glass chambers along the wall brightened a degree or maybe two, the colors inside them intensifying from unnamed to *felt*, and Ava's chest tightened with something adjacent to fear. Riley's tattoo flickered visibly, the lines contracting and expanding in time with the chambers' glow. Three things happening simultaneously, connected by a logic Ava could see but couldn't speak.

She looked at the camera. At the thousands of people watching.

"We might have family in the chat. Hi."

It was the most inadequate sentence she'd ever spoken and she knew it the moment it left her mouth. Then, quieter, not to the camera: "Riley."

Riley shook her head once. Not now.

The loop broke.

It happened all at once: Clara set down the clipboard with a clatter that was jarringly real, jarringly *now*, and turned to face them. Her eyes were clear, present. She looked at the camera on Ava's tablet and understood what it was with a speed that suggested this was not new information.

"The recipe was never about candy."

Her voice was precise, clipped.

"The emotional yield data in the personnel files: that's the actual product. Robert filed an internal complaint on September 14th. I tried to corroborate." She looked at the testing equipment cycling behind her, still running. "This equipment is still active. It's still measuring. Every person who enters this room—"

She stopped and looked at Ava. Directly at her, not through the camera but *at* her, and Ava felt the gaze land with physical weight.

"You see the structure of it. In your drawings. That's why it's watching you."

The sentence sat between them. Ava didn't breathe.

Clara's attention shifted; urgent now, the clarity already fraying at its edges, her fingers twitching toward the clipboard on the counter. "Don't go through the production line door. Tell the one with the camera… the boy who knows the building. He should not go near the wrapping machines."

The machinery in the wall cycled again. Louder, insistent.

Clara reached for the clipboard. Her hand closed around it and the pen was in her other hand before the motion completed and she was writing again. Down, across, up, flip, and her eyes were flat and her posture was perfect and the sixty-year loop closed around her like water filling a glass.

> **CandyKid_98:** *she warned you. please listen to her.*

> **CandyMan_1963:** *Quality assessment complete. Processing queue: updated.*

> **ViewerAlex:** *i just got another prompt to install that efficiency protocol extension. it says my "engagement level qualifies me for enhanced content." i'm not installing it but it won't stop asking.*

> **TechieTom:** *@ViewerAlex DO NOT INSTALL. i've been running packet analysis on that extension. it's pulling emotional response data from viewer devices.*

Nobody on screen saw the TechieTom message. Ava was looking at Clara.

Riley's voice was very controlled. "Her great-great-grandchild is watching the stream right now." She paused. "That's—"

She didn't finish.

Thomas was holding the door open. He'd moved to it during Clara's warning. Ava registered this now, belatedly, the way you notice an edit in a film only on second viewing. He'd heard it. *The one with the camera. The boy who knows the building.* His face was carefully composed.

"We should go," he said.

They went. Thomas led, back into the quality control corridor, away from the production line door where the light still leaked from beneath. Riley walked close to Ava, the file pressed against her chest, her wrist hidden under her sleeve now. She hadn't spoken since the unfinished sentence.

Ava looked at her sketchpad app. It had generated something during Clara's clarity window. She could see the new thumbnail in the gallery, timestamped three minutes ago. She opened it.

A diagram. Technical, precise, and rendered in the same impossible detail as the three images from before she'd entered the factory. The same diagram she'd half-recognized on Clara's clipboard, the processing routes and flow charts.

The app had labeled it with text she didn't input.

PROCESSING ROUTE: SUBJECT THOMAS MARTINEZ.
SEQUENCE: INITIATED.

She closed the app. She didn't show it to Thomas.
They walked.

***

The production line was operational.

That was the wrong word. The production line was *running*: conveyor belts grinding forward at walking pace, wrapping arms cycling through their stations in mechanical repetition, mixing vats turning with the wet patience of something that had never been asked to stop. Candy in colors that hurt to look at flowed through transparent pipes overhead, connecting vat to belt to wrapping station in a circulatory system the building wore on the outside.

Thomas had brought them through the maintenance corridor. The side route Clara had indicated during her clarity window, a service passage that opened onto the factory floor from an oblique angle, between two defunct cooling units. Less immediately dangerous, he'd said. Ava was starting to understand the precision of that phrasing.

"Stay to the left wall," Thomas said. His voice was pitched to carry over the machinery noise without shouting. Practiced. "The conveyor path runs center to right. There's a clearance corridor along the left that maintenance workers used. It connects to the east wing about two hundred meters up."

He knew the distances. He knew the layout like someone who'd walked it more than a hundred times, in the dark and in the impossible fluorescent light and in every state of the building's moods. Ava noted it and kept moving.

The noise was enormous, *consuming*. An overlapping percussion of metal on metal, belt on roller, arm on pivot, that filled the space so completely it became its own kind of silence. Ava's tablet was picking up the stream audio and she could see the waveform spiking into red. The chat would be getting a wall of industrial sound.

"Chat, can you hear us okay?" She held the tablet higher. "We're on the production floor. The machinery is active. I don't know why it's active. Thomas says—"

She stopped.

On the right side of the production line, a wrapping arm completed its downward cycle and paused. Not the mechanical pause of a programmed stop. A *held* pause, the way a head turns to track movement. Then it continued, but the angle of its return arc had shifted. Three degrees, maybe four. Toward Thomas.

Ava was an artist. She saw composition before content. Light, shadow, angle, weight. The wrapping arm's shift was a compositional break. A line in the frame that pointed somewhere it hadn't pointed before.

She kept walking, watched the next wrapping station from the corner of her eye.

Same thing. The arm cycled down, paused, adjusted its arc. Toward Thomas.

"Chat, the machinery on the right side. Is it moving? Like, actively?"

ShadowWatcher99: *YES it's tracking the guy with*

the vhs camera

FilmNerd_404: *the wrapping arms are rotating on their mounts. they're following him.*

StreamFan23: *thomas get away from the conveyor belt THOMAS*

CandyMan_1963: *Wrapping sequence: initiated. Subject identified. Analog documentation: priority acquisition.*

Ava read the first two aloud. She didn't read the CandyMan message; she was already moving. "Thomas—"

"I know." He didn't look at the wrapping arms. His camcorder was up, filming the overhead pipes where the emotional colors flowed. "I've known since we came through the door."

Riley was behind them both, the file still pressed to her chest. Her flashlight swept the wrapping stations and Ava saw her register the tracking. The subtle, synchronized adjustment of every arm on the right side, all of them oriented toward Thomas like flowers toward sun. Riley's jaw tightened.

"How far to the east wing connection?" Riley asked.

"Hundred and forty meters. Give or take."

"Then we move fast."

They moved. The left-wall corridor was narrow and cluttered with maintenance detritus: tool carts, oil drums and coiled electrical cable, and they wove through it in single file. Thomas first. Ava second, tablet held high, streaming. Riley last, watching behind them.

The wrapping arms followed. Every station they passed, the same adjustment. Down, pause, shift, continue. The machinery didn't speed up, didn't reach for him. It just *watched*.

Thomas stopped filming.

Ava almost missed it. The camcorder had been a constant: recording since the moment she'd met him, the red light on its body a steady companion in every corridor. He lowered it now. Held it in both hands, looking at it the way you look at something you're about to give away.

"Riley."

Riley came forward. Thomas held out the camcorder.

"Your great-grandfather tried to file a report. It got buried." He looked at the camera, then at Ava's tablet. The stream, the thousands watching. "This doesn't get buried."

Riley took it. Her hands closed around the plastic housing and Ava saw the weight of it register. The VHS tape inside. Twenty-eight years of footage no one had ever seen.

"Thomas—"

"That door." He pointed ahead, where the maintenance corridor terminated at a heavy steel door marked EAST WING ACCESS. "Don't stop."

Then, quieter, in the voice of someone who had been rehearsing: "I've been here since October '97. I've had a long time to figure out the route."

The camcorder shifted on his shoulder. It *tipped*. Gently, as if a child's hand had lifted the strap. Thomas reached for it reflexively, his body turning toward the conveyor belt, and the belt took it. Smoothly. The camcorder rode the rubber surface toward the first wrapping station with the unhurried pace of a product entering its designated line.

Thomas's hand stayed extended. His face went very still.

He understood.

Ava saw the understanding arrive. The last question answered.

He pushed them. Both hands, one on Ava's shoulder, one on Riley's, driving them toward the east wing door with a force that was controlled and final.

"*Go.*"

The wrapping arms extended.

Ava kept the camera up. She didn't decide to. Her hands held the tablet because her hands didn't know what else to do, and filming was what she did, and so she filmed. Thomas, from behind, moving toward the machinery. The wrapping arms reaching with the same measured cycling they'd been performing all along except now they had what they'd been cycling for. The moment of contact.

She couldn't describe it later. The arms wrapped and Thomas was there and then he was part of the line, incorporated into the process with an efficiency that made her stomach lurch because it was so *smooth*. So practiced. The machinery didn't strain, didn't adjust. It had been ready for this since 1997.

> *NightOwl_Explores: NO NO NO*
>
> *CandyKid_98: he's being pulled in oh god*
>
> *StreamFan23: is this real? is this actually happening?*
>
> *TechieTom: stream analytics just spiked. 47,000 concurrent viewers. the factory's using this. it's feeding off the viewer reaction.*
>
> *CandyMan_1963: Documentation: complete. Analog protocols: integrated. Welcome, Thomas Martinez, to permanent record.*

One second of silence. Every belt, arm, and vat paused for exactly one second, as if the system were swallowing. Then everything resumed at exactly the same rhythm, the same speed, as if nothing had been added and nothing lost.

In the overhead pipes, a new color joined the flow. Ava's brain reached for it. Copper. No. Bronze. No. It was the feeling you get when you almost remember something important, and it slid through the transparent tubing with the same unhurried pace as everything else.

Thomas's VHS camera was on the floor, intact. It had fallen, or been placed, off the conveyor belt near the base of wrapping station seven. Its viewfinder screen was lit, playing footage. Not the footage Thomas had shot. It was the factory in full operation, 1963, people in white uniforms moving between stations. They were smiling, all of them. The factory had made them look happy.

Riley picked up the camera. She held it to her chest with both arms in the same way she held the personnel file. Her tattoo was visible on her wrist, blinking with that new copper-bronze light. She didn't speak.

Ava looked at the chat because she didn't know where else to look.

> ***CandyKid_98:*** *i'm so sorry. i'm so sorry i recognized her. i'm sorry you were there.*

> ***StreamFan23:*** *i can't stop watching. i know i should turn it off and i can't stop watching.*

> ***TechieTom:*** *@StreamFan23 that's the point. that's what it wants. viewer count just hit 50k. every spike feeds it.*

Ava read TechieTom's message aloud. Her voice didn't sound like her voice. "Viewer count hit fifty thousand. Every spike feeds it."

She looked at the camera. At the fifty thousand people on the other side of the screen, watching from their beds and their desks and their phones, unable to look away for the same reason she was unable to put the tablet down.

"Turn it off," she said.

She didn't turn it off.

They didn't turn it off.

The count climbed.

Riley was already at the east wing door. She held it open with one hand, Thomas's camera pressed against her chest with the other. Ava walked through, the door closed behind them.

The corridor was quiet. There was still the distant hum of the building's systems, the faint vibration underfoot. Nothing active. Nothing tracking.

The comms crackled.

Carter's voice, bright with the specific enthusiasm of someone who had not been in the room: "Check-in. Everything okay over there? Your viewer numbers just went *insane*."

Ava looked at Riley. Riley looked at the VHS camera.

"Not okay," Ava said. "We're coming to you. Clara said—" she paused, organized what Clara had told them, kept her voice level for the stream. "Clara said there's something in the special ingredients storage we need to find. And she said—" she stopped again. "She said the factory is using the stream. Actively. The viewer count is part of it."

Static from Carter's end. Then: "How many viewers do we have right now?"

Ava didn't answer. The count was at 61,000. It was still climbing.

4

The server room was warm.

That was the first wrong thing. Every space in this building had carried the same damp chill, the cold of concrete that hadn't known climate control in decades. But the utility passage opened into a room that hit Evan with a wall of dry heat, the unmistakable exhale of active electronics running at capacity. His skin prickled with the temperature shift. His breath, which had been fogging since the loading dock, stopped.

He stood in the doorway and let his equipment tell him what he was looking at.

Server racks. Actual server racks, industrial-grade, floor-mounted in two rows of six. Behind them, older hardware: data processing units with toggle switches and paper-tape readers, a terminal array with CRT monitors casting green light across the floor. And behind *those*, running along the ceiling in original 1927 conduit, copper cabling thick as his thumb that fed into junction boxes which fed into the server racks. Which fed into, he traced the path with his eyes, thick modern-gauge cables that snaked across the concrete floor and disappeared into the wall toward the production floor.

All of it running, all of it powered. No generator hum, no electrical panel. No visible source.

"Okay so," Evan said, and then stopped, because the sentence he'd been constructing: *okay so this shouldn't exist*, was inadequate to the point of being insulting.

Carter was behind him. Camera up, framing the room over Evan's shoulder. His voice was the voice Evan had heard a thousand times, pitched for the audience and cadenced for engagement, but there was something thinner in it now. "Chat, you seeing this? We followed the signal into what appears to be some kind of server room. Evan, talk us through what we're looking at."

Evan set his laptop on the nearest flat surface, a cable spool that served as a table, and opened his network diagnostic suite. "Give me a second."

"Take your time. Chat, while Evan works his magic—"

"Carter."

Carter stopped.

"Just. Give me a second."

The diagnostic loaded. The local network appeared on his screen like a circulatory system rendered in neon. Too much traffic. He'd been monitoring their stream's network behavior all night, watching the anomalies accumulate like sediment. The 19.63-second packet drops. The metadata timestamps that read 1963. He'd cataloged them, rationalized them, filed them under *investigate later*.

Later was now.

The routing tables unfolded across his screen and Evan felt his stomach do something very specific. He recognized the protocol architecture from his coursework. From a networking history class he'd taken as an elective.

NCP. Network Control Protocol. The backbone of ARPANET before TCP/IP replaced it in 1983. Museum technology. Textbook footnotes.

It was running the factory's entire processing infrastructure.

He pulled up the node map. Each server rack was a node. The 1970s terminals were nodes. The production floor machinery somehow also impossibly registered as nodes. And beyond the factory's walls, extending outward through their streaming connection, sixty-one thousand viewer endpoints glowed like stars at the edges of the map.

"Evan." Carter had moved closer. He was reading over Evan's shoulder, which he always did, which Evan usually ignored. "What am I looking at?"

"A network map."

"Yeah, I got that. Why does it look like a… like a nervous system?"

Because it was one. Evan didn't say that. He traced a signal path from a viewer node in, the geolocation said Milwaukee, through their streaming platform's servers. Into the factory's network backbone, and down into the production floor. The path was bidirectional. Data flowed both ways; the viewers were connected to the processing infrastructure at the packet level.

"Chat's going to love this," Carter said, angling his camera toward the laptop screen.

He was right. He was also missing the point. Evan didn't have the words for what the point was yet, so he kept mapping.

The cables on the floor pulsed. He'd been refusing to think about that rhythm. Now in this room, with his diagnostic suite finally receiving clean data, he let himself measure it. He tapped a tempo counter on his phone and held it near the thickest cable bundle.

Forty-seven BPM.

The same tempo as the machinery on the production floor. The same tempo as Clara's clipboard rhythm, pen on paper, down-across-up-flip. The building's heartbeat. He'd clocked it in the parking lot, hours ago, when his equipment first started behaving strangely. He'd told himself it was electrical interference from the power grid.

There was no power grid connection. There hadn't been one since 1964.

Carter was reading the chat. His voice shifted into the patter he used when messages were coming fast.

"HauntHunter_Sarah says, hold on—"

> ***HauntHunter_Sarah:*** *After what happened I pulled every urban explorer report I could find for this location. There have been SIX documented groups who entered with streaming or filming equipment. None came out.*

> ***FilmNerd_404:*** *that tracks with the network load pattern — system's been doing this since at least 2008 based on forum archives*

> ***CandyKid_98:*** *my family tried to report Clara's disappearance for years. nobody would investigate. the factory was "decommissioned." there were no records of active operations.*

> ***CandyMan_1963:*** *All documentation is accurate and complete.*

Carter read HaunerHunter_Sarah's message aloud. Read FilmNerd_404's. Paused on CandyKid_98's. "Six groups. That's—" He scrolled past CandyMan_1963 without reading it. Evan watched him do it. Carter's thumb moved over that message the way a hand moves away from a hot surface: not a decision. A reflex.

A new message appeared. Evan saw it before Carter did.

> ***TechieTom:*** *evan — if you're in the server room, check the NCP routing tables. the system is using 1970s ARPANET protocol architecture. that's deliberate design. someone built modern processing capacity on top of a 50-year-old network backbone specifically so it couldn't be shut down by modern tools.*

Carter read it, frowning. "What's NCP routing?"

Evan was already pulling up the routing tables. TechieTom was correct.

Someone had built an interpreter with a sophistication that made Evan's chest tight.

He turned to the camera. He almost never did that. The camera was Carter's instrument, not his. But sixty thousand people were on the other side of that lens and one of them had just demonstrated expertise that Evan needed.

"TechieTom. Are you still in the chat? What else do you know about this architecture?"

The question cost him something. Not pride exactly. Something adjacent. The admission that the system he was looking at exceeded his ability to decode it alone. He watched the chat scroll, waiting.

While he waited, he ran the correlation. Viewer count against processing load. It was there. Clean, proportional, undeniable. When the count went up, the processing signatures in the server room intensified.

The factory had been expanding. Every stream, every viewer. Every engagement event. Building capacity toward something that required this scale.

"Carter."

Carter lowered his camera slightly. A rare gesture.

"More viewers means more of whatever it's doing with them. The processing load scales linearly with viewer count. I can see the math." He pointed to his screen. "This isn't incidental. The stream is *feeding* the factory."

Carter's face did something complicated. The content creator heard *the stream is feeding the factory* and filed it as narrative gold. The other thing behind his eyes that had been quietly assembling since the comms crackled and Ava said *not okay,* heard it differently. For a second, the two processes were visible simultaneously.

"So more viewers means—"

"More of whatever it's doing with them. Yes."

Carter looked at the camera. He looked at the view count: 63,400 now, still climbing. He looked at the camera again.

He didn't narrate.

The silence lasted three seconds. In streaming terms, an eternity.

> **TechieTom:** *i can see the load correlation from the outside too. every major emotional event in the stream spikes the processing signature by about 3-4%. thomas was a 31% spike.*

Evan read it quietly. He didn't read it aloud.

Carter, reading over his shoulder, did. "Thomas was a thirty-one percent spike." The words fell into the warm air. A man's life, converted to a metric. The number sat in the room between them like something physical.

"We should tell the others," Carter said.

"Tell them what exactly?"

Carter started composing a comms message. Stopped. Started again. His fingers hovered.

Evan leaned closer to his laptop. Something new was happening on the network map. A data stream, structured and deliberate, routing toward his equipment from deep inside the factory's maintenance systems. A *pattern*.

He recognized the error-correction protocol. It was his own; not literally, but functionally identical to the error-correction methods used in modern hybrid systems. Except this signal was coming from inside the 1970s terminal array. Someone had built a workaround: old infrastructure, modern communication format.

That required understanding of both systems. Which meant whoever, or whatever, was generating this signal had been in the factory long enough to learn both.

> **TechieTom:** *evan are you receiving anything on your*

> *error-correction channel? i'm seeing outbound structured data from the server room node on the network map*

Evan turned to the camera again. Twice in one day. A record.

"Yes. I am. I don't know what it's saying yet." He swallowed. "Chat, if anyone has experience with hybrid analog-digital error correction protocols from the late seventies, I need you in my replies right now. Seriously."

The cables flickered at forty-seven BPM. The structured signal intensified, as if something in the walls had heard him asking and was trying harder.

The ozone smell sharpened. A change in air quality, chemical and close, like standing next to a transformer that was being asked to carry more than it was built for. Evan's equipment hummed on a frequency he felt in his teeth.

He looked at Carter. Quietly and pitched beneath the stream audio: "If we stay live and something happens to one of us, that's a spike. That feeds it. Do you understand what I'm saying?"

Carter's jaw worked. "Yeah." Long pause. The green light from the CRT monitors played across his face. "I understand."

He didn't turn the stream off. Neither of them expected him to.

The comms crackled. Ava's voice, flat with the specific affectlessness of someone performing function because function was all that was left: "Coming to you. We lost Thomas. Clara warned us about the production line door. The viewer count—" a pause, breath, control. "Evan, the viewer count spiked when it happened. Fifty thousand people watched."

"I know," Evan said. "I have the data."

Carter, covering, the patter returning but wrong now, the rhythm off: "We're all okay over here. Mostly. Comms check: Derek, Maddie, Riley?"

On Evan's screen, the structured signal from the maintenance systems surged. Processing load spiked three percent. Something in the network knew the group was converging.

***

The signal led them down.

Not metaphorically. The structured data stream on Evan's tablet pulsed stronger as they moved through a doorway behind the server racks, into a corridor that dropped at a shallow grade. The walls changed. Gone were the painted cinderblocks and retrofitted conduit of the server room. Here was the original building — 1927 brick, rough-cut and sweating faintly, pipes bolted to the ceiling with stenciled labels in paint too old and flaked to read. The air tasted different. Mineral. Old water and older stone.

"This is giving strong catacombs energy," Carter murmured, camera sweeping the corridor. "Chat, we're following a signal Evan picked up from the maintenance systems. Heading deeper into the original structure."

Evan barely heard him. The signal was strengthening with every step, the error-correction handshake clean and deliberate, and his diagnostic suite was mapping the source to a point forty meters ahead and twelve meters below their current elevation. Whoever was sending this had been broadcasting into nothing for years. Maybe decades. The signal bore the hallmarks of extreme iteration; the same basic message refined and retransmitted thousands of times, each version slightly more efficient than the last. Someone had been practicing.

The corridor opened.

A maintenance bay. Workbench along the left wall, pegboard above it, tools hanging on pegs in an arrangement so precise it looked curated. Wrenches by size. Screwdrivers by head type. A voltmeter from the mid-seventies, its needle resting at zero, its case polished. In the corner, a portable generator hummed — a Honda E300, 1974 model if Evan's memory served, running at a steady idle that was the most ordinary sound he'd heard in this building. Someone had been feeding it fuel. Someone had been changing its oil. The air filter looked recent.

"Evan." Carter's voice had dropped. He was pointing his camera at the workbench.

Evan saw it. A logbook, open, filled with handwriting in neat block capitals. The visible page was dated. He stepped closer.

MARCH 14, 2024.

Two months ago.

The entries were maintenance logs. Generator runtime, fuel consumption. Server rack temperatures and cable insulation integrity checks. The handwriting was steady and practiced, the entries of a professional technician performing routine tasks on a very long schedule. Evan flipped back. 2023. 2019. 2011. 2003. The same handwriting. The same tasks. He flipped further. The pages yellowed.

NOVEMBER 8, 1974.

First entry:

> *Arrived to assess salvage potential. Generator*
> *operational. Initial survey of electrical systems.*
> *Noted anomalous power draw from production floor.*
> *Investigating tomorrow.*

There was no entry for tomorrow. The next entry was dated three weeks later, and the handwriting was different; shakier, the block capitals slightly irregular, as if the hand holding the pen had been re-calibrated.

> *Still here. System attempted full integration.*
> *Resisted. Maintaining generator. Someone will come*
> *eventually.*

Fifty years of maintenance logs. Evan's hand was trembling slightly when he set the book down.

"Carter. Film this page."

Carter moved in. Read the first entry aloud, then the second. His voice did something Evan had never heard it do: it got smaller.

The speaker on the wall clicked.

"That took you longer than I expected."

The voice was clear enough on the first six words, then the last three arrived from a second speaker farther down the corridor, as though the sentence had been routed through a junction and split. Male. Middle-aged. The flat affect of someone who had been alone long enough that speaking aloud had become a mechanical exercise rather than a social one.

Carter swung the camera. Evan looked.

He was there. At the far end of the workbench, leaning against the wall with his arms crossed. Or he was standing near the generator. Or he was both, the eye resolving him differently depending on the angle. Denim overalls. Union patch on the left sleeve, Local 47. Shaggy hair, significant sideburns. A face that looked forty, maybe forty-five, except that in peripheral vision the jaw dissolved into conduit and the fingers resting on his forearms were threaded with copper wire that ran into the wall behind him.

Evan looked directly at him. He solidified. Just a man, standing in a room he'd maintained for half a century.

"Michael Chen," Evan said.

"That's what it says on the union card." Through the speaker. His mouth moved but the sound came from the wall. He seemed used to the disconnect. "Your error-correction work is solid, by the way. Took me about six years to build the workaround, and you decoded it in twenty minutes. Different era."

ShadowWatcher99: he's partially translucent. can anyone else see that or is it my stream quality

*FilmNerd_404: not your stream. i can see it too. he's
not fully — he's not all the way here*

*TechieTom: thermal signature through the camera is
showing partial... this is going to sound insane:
partial integration with the wall infrastructure. he's
not a ghost. he's a hybrid.*

Evan read TechieTom's message aloud. Michael nodded slightly. The motion was human. The shadow it cast was not; it lagged a half-beat behind, tethered to the pipes.

"Hybrid is fair," Michael said, through the corner speaker. "I'm whatever you call someone who's been half-processed for fifty years because the system couldn't finish the job."

A silence. Carter's camera didn't waver, but his breathing had changed; shorter, held between sentences. Evan could hear him running the mental edit: *cut to Michael, hold on the tools, back to Michael.* Still working. Good. Evan needed Carter working.

"It wasn't a kindness," Michael added. His tone was the gallows variety. Flat, informational, the humor of five decades to sand the edges off the horror. "It kept trying. I got better at resisting. After a while we reached an equilibrium. I maintain the infrastructure. It leaves me enough of myself to do the job." He looked at his hands. The copper threads caught light. "Most days that's enough."

Evan set his tablet on the workbench. The signal he'd been following was originating from the junction box behind Michael, the conduit that ran through the wall and into the server room, from all of it simultaneously. Michael *was* the maintenance system, or enough of it that the distinction had become academic.

"You built the signal workaround," Evan said. "You've been trying to communicate."

"For six years. Since I figured out how the streaming signal worked. Watched four groups come through with cameras before you. None of them had the equipment to pick up what I was sending." He paused. The generator hummed. "You're the first ones who could hear me."

> *TechieTom: michael chen. maintenance worker, 1974. reported missing after an "industrial accident." OSHA investigation closed with no findings. company cited labor violations but was not shut down.*

> *HauntHunter_Sarah: there's a union newsletter from 1975 that mentions a worker named michael who "disappeared into the machinery." they meant it literally but nobody took it literally.*

> *HauntHunter_Sarah: Pulling the full missing persons record for this site. There are more. 1968: a journalism student named Margaret Sullivan. Filed a thesis proposal about the factory's closure that year. Her faculty advisor reported her missing five days into her fieldwork. Nobody connected it to the factory at the time. She was listed as a runaway.*

Carter read the messages aloud, clearly. Then, to Michael, with a quality of attention Evan had never seen from him on-stream: "Michael, the chat found your union records. HauntHunter_Sarah, TechieTom, he's here. He can hear you."

A beat. Carter's voice shifted, slightly awkward; the first genuine awkwardness Evan had witnessed from him in years of friendship. "Is that… okay? That they know?"

Michael looked at the camera. A lens. An audience. Fifty years of isolation, and now sixty-three thousand people could see him.

"I've been watching streams for six years," he said. "I know how this works."

The generator hummed. The tools on the pegboard hung motionless in their precise arrangements; the geometry of routine, of purpose preserved through repetition. Evan looked at the logbook. Fifty years. Every week, every oil change, every cable check and fuel-up. The most human thing in this entire building was a maintenance schedule kept by a man who was half-infrastructure.

"Michael." Evan's voice was steady. The steadiness cost him. "The signal you sent —"

"I was trying to tell you to stop the stream."

The words came through two speakers simultaneously. No fragmentation. Michael had put everything into making them land.

"The count is a processing queue. Every viewer is in the queue."

Evan felt the sentence reorganize something in his chest. Not surprise; the data had been pointing here. Hearing it stated by someone inside the system, stated as operational fact, was different from inferring it from network maps. He looked at his tablet. 67,200 viewers. 67,200 people in a processing queue they didn't know they'd entered.

Carter lowered his camera. Raised it again. Lowered it. The gesture was involuntary; his body trying to decide between documenting and responding.

"All of them?" Carter said.

"Everyone connected to the stream. The factory established the queue when your feed went live. Each viewer is tagged and assigned a position. The processing is sequential but it can batch. Right now it's running at capacity maintaining the queue. When it reaches threshold—" A speaker crackled. Michael's form flickered; for a half-second the man was gone and there was only conduit and junction boxes arranged in a vaguely human shape. Then he was back. "When it reaches threshold, it starts extracting."

> **HauntHunter_Sarah:** *processing queue. we're in a processing queue.*

> **TechieTom:** *running numbers. at current viewer count and processing rate, the factory could attempt mass-scale extraction within — i need more data. evan what's the load ceiling on the server room architecture*

> **StreamFan23:** *i should turn this off. i know i should turn this off. someone tell me to turn this off.*

> **CandyKid_98:** *i can't leave. i keep trying and i can't close the stream. the tab won't close.*

> **CandyMan_1963:** *Queue position confirmed. Processing sequence: optimal.*

Carter read the comments. He reached CandyKid_98's message and stopped.

His face changed.

"Chat. CandyKid, is the tab actually not closing? Can you tell me if that's happening to anyone else?"

The response was immediate. It was enormous. Messages cascading faster than Carter could track; dozens, then hundreds of viewers reporting the same thing. The stream tab wouldn't close. Force-quitting the browser reopened it. The stream auto-played on reopening. The volume reset itself. The chat scroll locked to the bottom. Evan watched Carter's eyes move as he read.

Carter read pieces of it aloud.

"Multiple viewers confirming. The tab won't close. Force-closing the browser doesn't work. The stream is—" He looked at Evan. "It's holding them."

"Closing it from your side doesn't remove you from the queue," Michael said. "Only active disconnection from the factory's end can do that. The system designed it that way. It learns from every interface upgrade. Your platform's features; it reverse-engineered all of it. Used it. The queue is maintained through the stream architecture itself."

Evan's mind was already three steps ahead, building the framework. "So we can't just kill the feed."

"Kill the feed and the queue persists. Every tagged viewer stays tagged. The factory processes them through residual connection; browser cache, cookies, device signatures. Slower, but functional. I've seen it happen."

"Then how—"

"Controlled termination. You broadcast a specific signal through the stream architecture that force-ejects every viewer simultaneously. Breaks the tag. Clears the queue." Michael pointed. Through the wall. Deeper. "The broadcast node is in special ingredients storage. That's where the stream originates from the factory's side. That's where it's always been."

> **TechieTom:** *ok. ok. evan. carter. listen. if the queue is real and forced disconnection is the only exit, the factory needs the stream live to maintain queue integrity. like he said, if you can create a controlled stream termination you could potentially force-eject all viewers simultaneously. it would require access to the factory's broadcast node. where is the broadcast node.*

Evan read it aloud. Looked at Michael. "So, special ingredients storage?"

"Everything runs through there. The processing, the queue, the broadcast." Michael's voice came through three speakers now, the sentence distributed across the room like a chord. "It's the heart of it."

Carter was still holding the camera. He looked at the viewer count: 78,000 and climbing.

He turned the camera to face himself. Carter Jameson, twenty-four years old, dark circles under his eyes, the green light of the CRT monitors reflecting off skin that was pale and slightly damp.

"Okay. Chat." His voice was unsteady. He let it be unsteady. "I need everyone who can hear this to listen. If you can't close the stream, stay with us. We're going to find the broadcast node. TechieTom, I need you on point with us. HauntHunter_Sarah, if you find anything else about the factory layout, keep it coming." He swallowed. "We're going to get you out of this."

He meant it. Evan could hear that he meant it in the way the sentence ended without an upturn, without the reflexive performative tag, without the *trust me* that usually punctuated Carter's promises.

The viewer count climbed. 82,000. 85,000. Carter watched the number rise and Evan watched Carter's face as the promise he'd just made became exponentially harder to keep with every new viewer who clicked in, drawn by the shares, the clips, the algorithm serving the stream to exactly the kind of curious, engaged audience the factory had been waiting for.

Carter turned the camera back to the room. His jaw was set. His hands were steady.

On Evan's tablet, the viewer count ticked past 89,000. A new message from TechieTom appeared at the bottom of the chat:

> **TechieTom:** *load threshold analysis: at current rate, the factory reaches processing capacity in approximately 90 minutes. that's your window.*

Carter read it aloud to the room. To the comms. To eighty-nine thousand people who couldn't look away.

Nobody argued with the number.

The comms crackled. Ava's voice: "We're close. Two minutes out. Riley has Thomas's camera. She's not letting go of it."

"Copy," Carter said. Then, to the comms, pitched for the group: "When you get here, we have a plan. Sort of. We have a destination and a ninety-minute window and a guy who's been stuck in the walls since 1974. I'll explain when you're here."

Michael, from the speaker nearest the door, quiet: "The factory knows you know. It's been listening to this conversation."

Evan looked at him. "I know."

"Move fast. It's going to start accelerating the queue."

They moved.

***

The door to special ingredients storage opened because Michael told it to.

The lock disengaged with a clean electronic click; a maintenance override routed through conduit that was part infrastructure, part person. The heavy steel door swung inward on hinges that someone had oiled within the last month.

The cold hit first.

Not damp cold or basement cold. The kind of temperature that existed because something needed to be kept. Evan felt it on his teeth before his skin registered it, a chemical sharpness that bypassed the nerve endings in his hands and went straight for the soft tissue of his throat. His breath came out visible. Carter's camera fogged for three seconds before the lens adjusted.

"Okay so," Evan said quietly. "New framework."

The room was industrial-scale large; a warehouse subsection with twenty-foot ceilings and fluorescent strips that activated in sequence as they entered, each one buzzing to life with a half-second delay, illuminating the space in a slow reveal that felt curated. Rows of floor to ceiling storage units lined both walls, sealed steel containers the size of filing cabinets with small glass inspection panels at chest height. Each one bore a label in a font Evan recognized immediately.

The Delightful Candy Co. house font. Rounded, cheerful, the kind of typeface designed to make children smile on packaging. Applied here to labels that read:

SUBJECT GROUP 1 — YIELD: 1963

SUBJECT GROUP 2 — YIELD: 1974

SUBJECT GROUP 3 — YIELD: 1988

Evan stopped walking. Carter didn't. Carter moved down the row with his camera, reading labels, and Evan watched him do it because it was easier than looking through the inspection panels.

He looked anyway.

The glass was thick and slightly distorted, but the contents were visible. Crystalline structures in colors he'd seen before: in the pipes on the production floor, in the liquid moving through the factory's circulatory system. Copper and rose and deep arterial red, solidified into geometric formations that caught the fluorescent light and held it. Beautiful, if you didn't know what they were. Each container held precise quantities, measured and labeled.

Behind him, footsteps. The rest of the group arriving through the corridor. Riley first, Thomas's VHS camera clutched against her chest like a talisman. Ava beside her, eyes already moving across the room in that particular way she had. Derek and Maddie close behind.

Maddie saw the labels. She stopped and pushed her glasses up. Pulled her phone from her pocket and snapped a photo of the nearest unit: Subject Group 5, 2008 without comment, without expression.

Riley saw Maddie photograph it. Her eyes tracked to the end of the row.

There it was. A storage unit with the same steel, same inspection panel and same cheerful font. The label read:

SUBJECT GROUP 7 — YIELD: [PENDING]

The date was this year.

Neither of them spoke. Riley's hand went to her wrist. Traced the tattoo. She heard Carter approach from behind her, probably to catch it in-frame.

> ***HauntHunter_Sarah:*** *subject group 7. that's you.*
> *they already made a container for you.*

> ***TechieTom:*** *the yield estimates on those containers*
> *— the quantities are impossible for five people. the*
> *viewer processing supplements the physical yield. the*
> *audience is part of the harvest.*

Carter read both messages aloud.

Silence. The fluorescents buzzed.

Derek, from the back of the group, his voice flat and dry and exactly right: "Right. So we definitely need to shut this down."

> *StreamFan23: YEAH WE DO*

> *ShadowWatcher99: DEREK FOR PRESIDENT*

> *CandyKid_98: please. please shut it down.*

The broadcast node was at the far end of the room.

Evan saw it and his brain did two things simultaneously: recognized the engineering and rejected the biology. The base structure was 1960s broadcast architecture with a signal tower framework and steel lattice, the kind of thing you'd find at a rural radio station. Built to transmit. Original to the factory. But over decades something had grown through it and around it, the way a tree's roots will slowly engulf a fence post. Modern hardware: routers, signal amplifiers, fiber-optic junctions. They had been integrated into the original frame by the same organic-mechanical process that had threaded copper wire through Michael's fingers.

It knew they were here. Evan could feel it as a measurable electromagnetic field that his tablet registered at 847 milligauss and climbing. The pressure behind his eyes was immediate and specific, the frequency of something not designed for human proximity.

"That's the node," Evan said. Unnecessarily. Everyone could feel it.

The screens activated.

There were six of them mounted at intervals along the wall nearest the node; old CRT monitors repurposed as display terminals, their surfaces dusty, their casings yellowed. They turned on in sequence, left to right, and the image that resolved on each was the same: a girl. Sixteen, maybe seventeen. Dark hair with colored streaks. Studded belt, band t-shirt, rubber bracelets on both wrists. A digital camera hanging around her neck. The image was sharp but wrong; the pixels were visible at the edges, the compression artifacts of someone who existed as data rather than matter.

She was trying to speak.

> **ViewerAlex:** *evan something is talking through the node. i can see it on the stream. the screens are showing a person but you can see the pixels aren't right*
>
> **TechieTom:** *digital ghost. more recent integration. 2000s by the compression artifacts in her signal.*
>
> **CandyKid_98:** *is she okay? is she — she looks scared*
>
> **HauntHunter_Sarah:** *Amber Wilson. 16 years old. Reported missing October 12th, 2007. Went to the factory with three friends for a photography project — said she was building her MySpace portfolio.*

Friends escaped. She didn't.

HauntHunter_Sarah: *Missing persons file listed her camera as never recovered.*

HauntHunter_Sarah: *She'd been documenting urban exploration sites for months before this one. Digital footprint goes cold the same night she disappeared.*

CandyMan_1963: *New inventory: registered. Processing queue: updated. Welcome, explorers.*

Carter was already looking at the screens when the last message appeared, already turning toward the Amber's image, and CandyMan_1963's message scrolled past unread.

The screens flickered. The image fragmented, pixels scattering like startled birds, then reassembled. Her mouth moved. Sound came, but not from the speakers. From the node itself. A vibration in the lattice structure that resolved into voice the way a tuning fork resolves into a note.

"Your — equipment — is better than ours was." The words arrived in bursts, each one costing visible effort against something pressing back. "We had cameras. Just cameras. The factory learned digital from — *us* —"

The screens scrambled. Went black. Came back. Amber's expression had changed; fury, clear and specific and completely human despite the pixelation.

"It's trying to shut me up. It does that." She pushed through. The screens brightened as if she'd shoved more power into them. "I can see the node architecture from inside. I can show you."

On the leftmost screen, the image shifted; the girl's face replaced by a schematic, rough but readable, the broadcast node's internal routing laid out like a circuit diagram. Evan stepped forward. His tablet was already syncing, already capturing.

> **ViewerAlex:** *she's trying to help. you can see it. she keeps redirecting the screen to show evan specific parts of the node*

> **TechieTom:** *she's routing diagnostic data through the screens. evan she's giving you a schematic*

"I see it," Evan said. "Amber? Can you hear me? I see the routing. Three primary junctions. The broadcast originates here but it's load-balanced across—" He traced the schematic with his finger. "Two secondary nodes. Where?"

The screens flickered again. Harder this time. The factory pushing back. Amber's image strobed between her face and static, the schematic wavering. She forced two words through before the suppression cut her signal to fragments:

"Production — floor —" Static. "— packaging —"

Then she was back, gasping as if the effort were physical, her digital form reassembling pixel by pixel.

"Three nodes. Sixty-second window. All three — simultaneously — or the queue redistributes and you lose everyone."

Evan's mind was already building it. Three locations. Three teams. Sixty-second synchronization window. The equipment they had: Carter's broadcast rig, Evan's diagnostic suite, the comms system. It could theoretically coordinate it. The power draw required to generate a force-eject signal strong enough to clear ninety-four thousand viewers meant pulling from the factory's own grid, which meant the factory would feel it, which meant—

"It'll fight back," he said aloud. Not a question.

"It'll fight back," Amber confirmed. The screens dimmed. She was losing ground. "But the architecture has to route the signal before it can respond. You get — maybe forty seconds — of uncontested broadcast before the defensive systems engage."

Evan turned to the group. All six of them, framed in the broadcast node's electromagnetic glow. Riley with Thomas's camera. Ava with her tablet, her fingers already moving across the screen in unconscious sketching motions. Derek positioned between the group and the storage units without having decided to. Maddie with her phone still out, data still recording. Carter with the camera aimed at Evan's face, waiting for the plan he could see forming.

"Three nodes," Evan said. "Production floor, packaging, and here. Three teams. We execute simultaneously within a sixty-second window…"

Maddie was already cross-referencing the schematic on her tablet. "The production floor node is at the convergence point. Center of the building, where the processing lines meet. Packaging is the administrative override; it's where the factory's original control infrastructure is housed. And here is the broadcast node." She looked up. "Different names depending on whether you're reading the building or the system."

Evan continued. "The signal has to be strong enough to force-eject the entire queue, which means we're drawing power from the factory itself. Which means it's going to know, and it's going to respond." He looked at Carter. "And someone has to stay here with the broadcast node and run the primary sequence while the factory is actively trying to stop them."

A beat. Carter didn't blink.

"I'll run the broadcast," Carter said. Simply. Without the pitch. Without the performance.

> **TechieTom:** *three-point simultaneous access. timing has to be exact. evan what's the coordination mechanism?*

> **HauntHunter_Sarah:** *i can track all three locations on the stream if you split the feed. carter you can broadcast all three simultaneously.*

Carter let out something that wasn't quite a laugh. "Chat's already planning logistics." He steadied. "Okay. TechieTom, HauntHunter_Sarah; you're our external team. Coordinate the timing from outside. We'll handle the physical nodes."

The screens flickered one final time. Amber, pushing through the factory's suppression with everything she had, held the schematic visible for three seconds. Evan's tablet captured it. Then static consumed her, the screens went dark, and the broadcast node hummed at a frequency that settled behind Evan's eyes like a migraine waiting to happen.

Viewer count on Carter's phone: 94,000.

Carter turned the camera to face the group. All of them, together, lit by the node's residual glow and the cold fluorescents and the faint luminescence from the storage units that held the yield of six previous groups and the empty container waiting for the seventh.

"Chat, this is the team. We have a plan. We have seventy minutes." He paused. "Thank you for staying with us."

He meant the watching audience. He meant the ones who couldn't leave.

Carter read the first two. Scrolled past the third.

Maddie noticed Robert check his watch, the same automatic gesture he'd made a dozen times tonight. She'd logged it each time without examining it. She examined it now.

"Mr. Morgan. Your watch."

Robert looked at it. "It's kept the same time since —" He paused. "Since I've been here."

The face read 19:63.

Maddie looked at her notes. The factory's countdown: *nineteen minutes, sixty-three seconds*. Evan's packet loss intervals from the first hour: *19.63 seconds*. The number the factory had been running on all night, embedded in every anomalous reading they'd logged.

"The factory's operational clock," she said. It came out quieter than she intended. "It's been running on your timestamp. The moment it processed you; that's the fixed point it's been anchored to."

Robert looked at the watch. At the frozen hands. At a reading that hadn't changed in sixty years.

"That would explain," he said, after a moment, "quite a lot."

He put the watch away. They kept moving.

They split. Carter and Evan at the broadcast node. Riley and Ava toward the production floor. Derek and Maddie toward packaging. The comms stayed open. Carter rigged the multi-feed with three cameras, three locations, one stream; HauntHunter_Sarah confirmed eyes on all three before the first pair reached the corridor.

As Derek and Maddie's footsteps faded, the factory's machinery which had been silent since Thomas, since the production line had taken him and the group had run; it began cycling again.

Deeper. Slower. More deliberate.

On the stream, a countdown appeared in the chat. Pinned to the top. TechieTom's doing. Nobody had asked him.

69:42

69:41

69:40

5

The corridor was wrong and Derek knew it before he could prove it.

Forty-seven steps from the last junction, he'd been counting. Old habit, football field pacing, the kind of spatial math his body did without consulting his brain. The blueprint Maddie had pulled up on her tablet showed this passage at forty feet, junction to junction. Standard factory service corridor. He'd walked forty-seven steps, which put him around sixty feet, and the next junction wasn't here yet.

He didn't say anything. Bad estimate. Tight corridors messed with your stride.

The three of them moved in formation without having discussed it: Derek on point, Maddie in the middle with her tablet casting blue-white light on the walls, Riley trailing by two steps with Thomas's VHS camera held against her sternum like body armor. The comms hummed with Carter and Evan's chatter from the broadcast node, distant and tinny. The factory's ambient sound had settled into something low and distributed, not a single machine running but the murmur of many small mechanisms doing many small things, like a building filling out paperwork.

"Next left," Maddie said. "Then straight through to the loading bay."

Derek took the left. The corridor extended. Brick walls, concrete floor, old plaster patching where pipes had been rerouted decades ago. Fluorescents overhead, half of them dead, the survivors casting flat institutional light that made everything look like a photograph of itself. Nothing dramatically wrong here.

He counted again. Fifty-two steps to a junction that should have been thirty feet away.

This time he noticed himself noticing and kept walking. Behind him, Riley's footsteps were steady and unhurried and she hadn't said a word since they'd split from the main group. Derek kept her in his peripheral awareness the way he kept exit routes in his peripheral awareness.

"Loading dock should be—" Maddie paused and pushed her glasses up. She looked at the tablet, then at the wall ahead. "Through there. One more junction."

They took the junction. The stenciled signage on the wall, original 1927 Delightful Candy Co. wayfinding, read **LOADING** → in faded but legible white paint. Derek followed the arrow; the corridor stretched. Brick, concrete, fluorescents. The same corridor. Different pipe configurations, different plaster patches, but the same *type* of corridor. It repeated with the persistence of a loading screen.

At the next junction, the arrow read **LOADING** → again.

Derek stopped. He looked back at the previous arrow, still visible twenty feet behind them. That one pointed right and this one pointed right. But the first right had been oriented toward the building's west wall, and this right was oriented slightly south of west.

The arrows weren't pointing to the same place.

He didn't say anything. Kept moving.

"Hmm," Maddie said, very quietly.

A window appeared on the left wall. It was small, industrial, wire-reinforced glass. Derek looked through it and his chest did something involuntary, because there it was: the loading dock. Concrete platform, steel roll-up doors, the yellow safety paint on the floor edges were still visible.

Close. Maybe fifty yards. Reachable.

"There," he said. "Straight shot."

The route to that window's side of the building required the next left turn. He took it. The corridor curved gently and deposited them at another junction with another stenciled arrow. **LOADING** →, pointing them away from the window. Away from the dock he'd just seen with his own eyes.

He stopped and looked at the arrow. Looked back at the corridor they'd just walked.

Riley was watching him. Had been watching him, maybe, the whole time. Her eyes tracked from his face to the arrow and back. She said nothing.

"The arrows are rotating," Maddie said. She'd pulled up something on her tablet and was swiping between screens. "Each junction, the directional indicators are shifting approximately seven degrees south. It's cumulative. If we keep following them, they'll route us in a—"

"Circle," Derek said.

"Spiral, technically. But yes."

Derek held the camera up. The red light was on — Carter had set it to continuous broadcast when they'd split. "Chat. We've been following the loading dock signs and they're not taking us to the loading dock. Anyone seeing this?"

He held the camera on the most recent arrow. Waited.

HistoryBuff_Marie: derek i've been mapping your route against the 1962 construction plans. you should have hit the loading dock six minutes ago. you're moving but the dock isn't getting closer.

TechieTom: corridor length discrepancy confirmed. passage you're in should be 40 feet. feed analysis shows you've walked at least 70.

Derek read them aloud.

Maddie was already pulling up her blueprint. She looked at it, then at the corridor. She said, very carefully: "The map says we're there."

Derek: "We're not there."

"No. We're not."

Riley looked at the floor.

Derek followed her gaze. His flashlight caught it at a low angle; barely visible in the flat overhead light, but readable once you knew to look. Candy wrapper residue. Fine, crystalline dust in faded pastels, the same residue that had been underfoot since the production floor. It traced a path along the corridor, and that path curved. Gently and incrementally. In a slow, deliberate arc that matched the arrow rotation exactly.

Not toward the loading dock.

Away from it.

"It's been pointing us wrong the whole time," Riley said. The first words she'd spoken since they'd left the broadcast node. Just that. Flat and certain and completely without surprise.

Derek looked at the camera. "Chat, I think the factory's running us in circles. Not like, horror movie circles. Like it doesn't want us to notice." He paused. "Has anyone seen this in the other groups' footage?"

and going by structural logic — following the exterior wall.

***HistoryBuff_Marie:** exterior walls run true even when interior layout is manipulated. structural load-bearing elements can't be relocated. find an exterior wall and follow it.*

Derek turned to Maddie. "We follow the wall."

"That's… yes. That's structurally sound." She was already turning, tablet angled to identify the nearest exterior-facing surface. Her free hand touched the brick to their right. "This one. Load-bearing. Exterior grade."

Riley was already moving. She put her hand on the wall and walked, and the wall: solid, real, indifferent to whatever the factory was doing with its interior geography. It led them forward without deviation. The corridors still stretched. The signs still pointed wrong. But the wall held true, and after two turns and a staircase that had seven steps instead of four, the loading dock appeared at the end of a passage and stayed where it was as they approached.

No elasticity. Just a space behaving like a space.

Derek clocked the time in his head. Twenty-six minutes gone. He didn't say it on stream.

"Loading dock," he said instead, scanning the space. There was the concrete platform, steel doors, the machinery already humming its low distributed hum. "Node two should be in the northeast corner. Chat, can anyone confirm the node location from the schematics Evan sent?"

***TechieTom:** northeast corner confirmed. behind the secondary freight elevator housing. 26 minutes elapsed. 44 remaining. you can still make this.*

Derek didn't respond. He kept moving.

***

The loading dock opened around them like a held breath finally released.

Derek swept the space in two passes. Concrete platform, waist-high. Steel roll-up doors along the western wall, all down, their chains rusted into fixed positions. Loading ramps with rubber bumpers cracked and peeling. A forklift parked mid-turn near the south wall, its forks raised and frozen at hip height, holding nothing. Pallets stacked against the far wall, some upright, some toppled in configurations that suggested they'd been rearranged more than once.

The smell here was different. Rubber and rust and cold concrete. It was industrial, honest, the most factory-like smell they'd encountered since entering the building. The ubiquitous sweetness was still present, but faint. Like it had traveled a long way to reach this corner of the building and arrived weakened.

"Northeast corner," Maddie said, already moving. "Behind the freight elevator housing."

Derek let her lead. His eyes were still working the space, cataloguing cover positions, sight lines, the distance from the platform edge to the nearest roll-up door.

The secondary freight elevator housing was a steel-walled enclosure bolted to the dock's northeast corner, its doors welded shut decades ago. Behind it, exactly where TechieTom had confirmed, sat the utility junction box. Industrial gray. Original hardware with the same organic-mechanical growth threading through its seams: newer wiring and fiber-optic tendrils, the factory's evolutionary integration visible in every joint.

But Derek had stopped looking at the junction box. Because next to it, tucked into the corner where the elevator housing met the exterior wall, someone had built a home.

Sleeping bag, military surplus by the look of it, rolled neat and tight against the wall. A wooden crate turned on its side, serving as a table. A tin cup sat on top near a stub of candle in a jar and a paperback with its spine cracked past repair. Photographs pinned to the brick above the sleeping bag hung in two careful rows, their edges curling but their placement deliberate. A transistor radio rested on the crate's lower shelf, olive drab with its dial lit gold and its speaker producing a low, steady hiss of white noise. The dial was taped in place with electrical tape gone brittle and brown. A record sleeve leaned against the crate: *London Calling*, The Clash, its cardboard soft with age.

Derek stared at all of it. The organization. The *system*.

"Someone's living here," he said.

Maddie had already crouched beside the crate. She was looking at the food storage: canned goods arranged by type on a shelf fashioned from a bent loading ramp bracket, water bottles filled from some source and dated in marker on their caps. Her hand came up to push her glasses and she made a small sound.

"This is—" she began. "The rotation system on the water supply alone… this person has been maintaining inventory in a way that would meet OSHA standards."

Riley hadn't moved. She was standing three feet from the photographs, Thomas's camera pressed against her chest, looking at the images pinned to the wall. Young people. A group photo outside a movie theater, everyone in denim and oversized jackets. A Polaroid of a girl with spiky purple hair flipping off the camera and laughing. Another of the same girl with an older woman, her mother probably, standing in front of a house with a garden.

1986. All of it. The clothes, the hair, the film stock.

Riley went still in the specific way Riley went still when something landed.

ShadowWatcher99: those photos on the wall. can you zoom? i want to see the dates.

> **StreamFan23:** *she's been living here. actually living here. for how long.*

> **CandyKid_98:** *the radio's on a shortwave frequency. she's been trying to call for help.*

Derek looked at the radio. Its golden dial glowed steady, tuned to a frequency that produced structured nothing.

He looked up.

The catwalk ran along the dock's upper perimeter, a steel-grate walkway that accessed the overhead crane mechanisms and ventilation systems. It was twenty feet up and mostly in shadow, the fluorescents below not reaching that high.

Someone was standing on it.

Derek's hand went to the scar above his eyebrow. He caught himself. Dropped it.

She was watching them the way you watch animals that have wandered into your territory; *assessing*. She stood at the catwalk rail with both hands resting on it, weight distributed evenly, positioned directly above the shelter with the ease of someone who had made this exact observation a thousand times before. Height advantage with clear sight lines. Multiple exits along the catwalk in both directions.

Not a person hiding.

Derek looked at her. She looked back. He could feel the calculation running behind her eyes; threat or resource. Fight or coordinate.

He said, to the catwalk rather than the camera: "We heard you."

It was the right thing to say. He didn't know it was the right thing to say until he said it.

A beat. She shifted her weight. Then she looked past Derek, past Maddie, to Riley. To the camera Riley was holding against her chest. The VHS camera. Thomas's camera.

"Where did you get that?"

Not aggressive. As if she recognized the object before she recognized the people holding it.

Riley looked up. Her hand tightened on the camera's body. "It belonged to someone we met inside. Thomas Martinez."

The girl didn't move for a moment. Then she gripped the catwalk rail, swung over it, and dropped twenty feet. She caught a support strut halfway down, redirected her momentum, and landed on the concrete dock floor with a sound like a single hand-clap. Clean and practiced, as if she'd made it a hundred times.

She looked like she was in her late twenties. Spiky hair that had once been purple, faded now to a dusty violet-gray. Clothes that had been repaired and re-repaired until they were their own thing. A jacket made of three jackets, combat boots with mismatched laces; one red, one black. Multiple earrings that caught the fluorescent light. She moved with coiled efficiency.

The woman looked at Derek and at Maddie for a brief moment. Then her gaze met Riley and the VHS camera and she went still.

"That's a GR-AX7," she said. "I've seen that camera before." There was a pause that lasted exactly long enough. "Where's the person who was carrying it?"

Derek answered straight with no cushioning. "The wrapping machines. On the production floor. About an hour ago."

The loading dock went quiet. Somewhere deep in the walls, behind the steel and concrete, something clicked. A pressure change, subtle as an ear popping. The sound of something rerouting.

She nodded once. "Wrapping machines?"

"Yeah."

"He'd been trying to find his crew since '97. I'm glad he found people before—"

She didn't finish. She picked up the thread of functionality instead. "What's the plan? You look like you have a plan."

Derek opened his mouth but the chat was already moving.

> **NightOwl_Explores:** *she's incredible. she's survived in there since THE EIGHTIES.*

> **HauntHunter_Sarah:** *jenny reeves. reported missing 1986. search party found nothing. her parents never stopped looking.*

> **CandyKid_98:** *can she hear us? does she know we're here?*

Derek lowered the camera so she could see the screen. "Jenny, there are about ninety-four thousand people watching this stream right now. They've been helping us navigate tonight."

Jenny stared at him, then at the camera. Then at Maddie's tablet, where the chat was scrolling, thousands of messages a minute, names and timestamps and a living wall of text.

"...Ninety-four thousand."

"They found the shelter before we did. And they know who you are."

Jenny looked at the camera for a long moment. The golden glow of the transistor radio caught the edge of her face. The static hissed its steady nothing.

Then, to the camera, to the ninety-four thousand people she couldn't see: "Did my parents watch this?"

It landed in the chat like a stone in still water. The scroll slowed. The responses took a moment.

> **HauntHunter_Sarah:** *i'll find out. i promise. i'll find out right now.*

StreamFan23: we're here. we've been here all night.

CandyKid_98: we see you.

Derek read all three.

Jenny watched the chat move on the tablet. She didn't say anything for five seconds,. Then she turned around and walked to the utility junction box with the brisk stride of someone who had been waiting a very long time for someone to show it to.

"This box has been bleeding power since before I got here," she said, tapping the housing with two knuckles. "I've been running my radio off the secondary circuit for years. The main lines go deep; into the walls, into the floor. Whatever's inside it hums louder when the machines are active." She looked at Maddie. "You want to document it before we open it?"

Maddie was already there, tablet raised, recording.

Derek keyed the comms. "Evan. We're at the node. And we've got someone you need to talk to."

He handed the earpiece to Jenny. Watched her hold it and examine it, the technology unfamiliar but the concept clear enough. She put it in her ear.

"This is Jenny. I've been living next to your junction box for about—" She paused. "A while. Tell me what you need."

Through the earpiece, Evan's voice. Then Jenny's responses which were immediate and technical. They established a rapport in thirty seconds flat.

The node was accessible. Evan walked Jenny through the first stage of the termination sequence prep. Maddie documented. Derek watched the dock entrance, positioning himself between the open space and the group without deciding to.

Time on the pinned countdown: 38:14.

From beyond the loading dock's eastern wall, audible through the steel and concrete, the production floor machinery shifted register. Something that had been running at one speed was now running slightly faster.

No one mentioned it.

***

The junction box hummed under Jenny's hands like something breathing.

Derek counted the lights. Three fluorescents overhead, all dead when they'd arrived. Now the first one farthest from the group, near the southern roll-up doors, flickered on. Emergency-dim.

He noted it. Kept his position at the dock entrance.

Maddie had her tablet propped against a pallet, split-screening between Evan's remote diagnostics and her own documentation feed. "Node prep at thirty-one percent," she said. "Evan says the handshake protocol is slower than the broadcast node; this one's deeper in the system."

"How much slower?"

"Eleven minutes to full prep completion." She pushed her glasses up. "Give or take."

Derek did the math against the countdown. Tight but workable. He adjusted his stance and watched the eastern corridor entrance. It was a wide freight passage that opened onto the dock's far end, its depth swallowed by darkness beyond the first fifteen feet.

The second fluorescent came on. Closer. Same dim quality, same reluctant ignition. It illuminated a section of catwalk above them that had been invisible before.

Jenny looked up from the junction box. Her hands didn't stop working; Evan's voice was a low murmur in her earpiece but her eyes tracked the light.

"It does that when it's orienting," she said.

Maddie: "Orienting toward what?"

"Whatever it's decided to look at."

Nobody asked the follow-up. The third fluorescent was already warming, directly above them now, its gold glow settling over the junction box and Jenny's hands and the neat military bedroll three feet away. The sequence was complete, ending at their position.

Derek's hand twitched toward his scar. He caught it. Redirected the energy into a grip adjustment on the camera.

Across the dock, near the eastern entrance, a loading arm. It was hydraulic, ceiling-mounted, dead steel for decades. It raised six inches. Smooth and slow, like something stretching after a long sleep. It stopped. Held. Then nothing.

Seven seconds later, a conveyor section along the east wall engaged. Three seconds of belt movement, the rubber cracked and protesting, carrying nothing. Then silence.

Both near the eastern entrance., both checking angles.

Riley was sitting against the elevator housing with Thomas's VHS camera held to her eye, the viewfinder's blue glow painting one side of her face. She'd been reviewing the footage quietly while the others worked. Her own camera sat beside her, still broadcasting.

Derek let her work. He scanned the eastern corridor again; dark and still. The loading arm hadn't moved again.

"Node at fifty-eight percent," Maddie said. Then, "Derek."

He turned.

She was looking at her tablet. Something was happening in the chat that had changed her posture, straightened her spine, brought her glasses-pushing hand up twice in three seconds.

"The chat is receiving a video feed," she said. "It's not from any of our cameras."

Derek crossed to her in four steps. On the tablet, embedded directly in the chat stream were still images. Analog grain, not digital compression. A factory floor, fully operational, with workers in period uniforms moving between production lines. The color palette of old security footage: washed greens and grays, high contrast and fixed angle.

The timestamp in the lower right corner read:

10/14/1963 — 02:47 AM.

The images began to move, frame by frame becoming fluid. The camera panning across the production floor, past the wrapping stations, through a doorway and into the loading dock. The 1963 loading dock. Same concrete platform and steel doors. The same freight elevator housing in the northeast corner, newer then, its paint intact.

And standing in the loading dock, visible in sixty-year-old security footage with a sixty-year-old timestamp: Derek. Maddie. Riley against the elevator housing. Jenny at the junction box. Their current positions, their current postures, captured from a high angle in the dock's upper right corner.

> *TechieTom: i don't know how to explain what i'm looking at. someone is sending 1963 security footage to the chat. the footage shows your current position. the timestamp is 1963. you are in it.*
>
> *NightOwl_Explores: how are you in 60 year old footage. HOW ARE YOU IN IT.*
>
> *ShadowWatcher99: look at the upper right corner of the dock. the camera that's showing this feed. is that camera physically there.*

Derek shone his light up.

In the upper right corner, where the eastern wall met the ceiling above the catwalk. Rusted housing, analog mount, a lens thick with decades of dust. A security camera so old it predated the factory's closure. It was bolted into the concrete with hardware that had oxidized to the color of dried blood.

On its underside, small and steady: a red light.

On.

The same model. The same red light he'd clocked on the exterior of the building when they'd first arrived. The detail Carter had framed for the stream's opening shot, that chat had flagged hours ago. The seed planted in the first minutes of the broadcast, growing here in the loading dock, sixty years deep.

Derek looked at the *factory's* camera, "It's been watching us since we came in."

Jenny didn't look up. "Since before you came in."

"Node at seventy-three percent," Maddie said. Her voice had the compressed staccato of Maddie-under-pressure, all verbs and no hedging. "Eleven minutes to hold completion."

Derek turned back to the chat. The security feed was still cycling in the stream: their position from the factory's eye, an angle that covered the entire dock including the eastern entrance and the corridor beyond it. An angle none of their cameras had.

He said it before thinking it through, because it was the correct move: "Chat, if you can see us on that feed, tell me what you see that we can't see from here."

Four seconds.

> **TechieTom:** *eastern entrance. there's something in the corridor beyond it. not moving but it's there.*
>
> **ShadowWatcher99:** *it looks like machinery but the profile is wrong. too irregular.*
>
> **HauntHunter_Sarah:** *jenny. jenny would know what that is.*

Jenny didn't look toward the eastern entrance. Didn't need to.

"It's a collection mechanism," she said. Her hands kept working the node.

Her voice was the voice of weather reports and bus schedules. "Factory sends them to doorways when it's corralling. It's not going to come in yet; it waits until you move."

Maddie: "So we don't move."

"We finish what we're doing. Then we move together, fast, through the north passage, not the east." She tilted her head toward a service door set into the dock's north wall, partially hidden behind the stacked pallets. "I've used it a hundred times. It connects to the maintenance tunnels. The collection mechanisms can't fit."

Riley lowered the VHS viewfinder from her eye.

Derek had been tracking her peripherally: the small movements of rewinding and playing, the way her breathing had changed ten minutes ago, the way it had changed again just now. Something in the footage had shifted.

"Evan." Riley's voice on comms. Flat and certain. "Thomas is in the system. He's trying to say something. I think he's trying to say something."

Derek looked at her. She was holding the camera's viewfinder angled so that Ava's camera, which was still broadcasting from its mount on Riley's pack, could catch the tiny screen. On it was footage that wasn't Thomas's. Angles that weren't physically possible. The factory from inside itself: corridors folding, machinery seen from within its own mechanisms, perspectives that bent wrong. And in one frame, held steady for half a second was Thomas. Standing, looking directly into the lens. His mouth forming a word.

> *CandyKid_98: we can see the viewfinder through ava's camera. frame by frame — he's saying "north passage."*

North passage. Three independent sources converged on the same answer from three different positions inside and outside the factory's architecture.

Derek read the last messages aloud. He read them to Jenny, specifically.

She looked at the VHS camera in Riley's hands, and the dusty violet of her hair caught the golden light.

"Stubborn," she said, with something that might be the ghost of a smile. "He was always stubborn."

"Node prep at ninety-one percent," Maddie said. "Four minutes."

Derek settled into the wait. The collection mechanism didn't move. The factory's camera watched from its corner, red light steady and patient. The interference had stopped escalating. The equipment stayed still. The dock existed in a held breath of mechanical silence that felt, if Derek had been the kind of person to articulate such things, like something recalculating.

He wasn't. So he watched the eastern entrance and he waited, and he kept his body between the corridor and his people.

"Node prep complete," Maddie said. "Evan confirms. We're done."

"North passage," Derek said. "Jenny leads. I'm last. We move now."

Jenny pulled the earpiece out, pocketed it, and crossed to the service door in four strides. She had it open before Derek finished the sentence; a steel door that swung inward on hinges she'd clearly maintained, revealing a maintenance tunnel lit by nothing at all.

She went through; Maddie followed. Riley paused at the threshold long enough to look back at the dock and the security camera. At the eastern entrance, at the space Jenny had lived in, and then she went through too.

Derek was last. He stepped through the door and pulled it shut behind him, the steel seating into its frame with a sound like a period at the end of a sentence.

Three seconds later, visible on ninety-four thousand screens but no one in the north passage, the collection mechanism entered the loading dock. It moved through the eastern entrance with the liquid patience of something that had expected to find them there. It found the junction box, the transistor radio still hissing its golden static, the sleeping bag rolled tight against the wall.

Empty.

> *NightOwl_Explores: it came in right after you left. three seconds.*

> *TechieTom: 28 minutes remaining. node two prep complete. all teams converging. you're on schedule.*

> *CandyMan_1963: Efficiency noted. Recalibrating approach parameters.*

The third message sat in the chat for eleven seconds before the first viewer flagged it. By then the group was deep in the maintenance tunnel, Jenny's combat boots steady on the concrete ahead, and the chat's unease rippled outward into a silence that nobody on stream would see.

6

The pipe tobacco hit her first.

Not the stale ghost of it, this was fresh. Sweet and sharp, the specific blend her grandmother had described a hundred times: cherry vanilla with something darker underneath, something earthy that Margaret Morgan said she could never find in any store because it wasn't a brand, it was Robert's own mix, and the recipe died with him.

Riley stopped in the doorway of the testing chamber and her hand went to her wrist before she could stop it.

The tattoo wasn't warm. The candy wrapper design on her inner wrist was *vibrating*, a low hum that she could feel in the bones of her hand, in her teeth, in the architecture of her inner ear. Like a tuning fork struck against the exact frequency of the room.

"Riley." Ava called from behind her, voice soft. "You feel that too, right? The air in here is... it's *thick*. Like the room is full of something I can't see."

"Yeah." Riley stepped inside. "I feel it."

The testing chamber was clinical in a way the rest of the factory hadn't been. White tile walls, stained but intact. A single subject station at the center of the room: an adjustable chair bolted to the floor, surrounded by a ring of monitoring equipment on wheeled carts, all of it analog and pristine. *Maintained.* Display cases along the left wall held candy samples in glass jars, organized by batch number in handwriting she recognized.

She recognized it because she'd grown up with it. In birthday cards her grandmother kept in a shoebox. In the margin notes of a journal she'd found at fourteen and read under her covers with a flashlight, heart hammering, understanding for the first time that the official story was wrong.

The journal was here, too.

Open on the heavy oak desk against the far wall. The desk was polished, with a green blotter and a rotary phone and a half-empty coffee mug that still had a ring of liquid inside it. Sixty years old and still wet. The aftershave arrived with the tobacco, layered underneath it: the brand's original formulation, the one they'd changed twice since. She knew because her grandmother had kept a bottle of it unopened in the bathroom cabinet for forty years, and Riley had unscrewed the cap once when she was nine and the smell had made her grandmother cry.

The factory was manufacturing nostalgia. and it worked. That was the horror of it.

Ava had her tablet up, the sketchpad app already running. "The app's generating on its own again," she said quietly. "Architectural overlays. It's… Riley, it's drawing faster than I can track."

"Document everything." Riley moved to the desk.

The journal was open to a page near the middle. The handwriting was Robert Morgan's. She'd know it across a room, across whatever membrane separated his time from hers. Precise block letters that slanted slightly left, the habit of a right-handed man who'd been taught penmanship by a left-handed mother. The pen pressure was even and controlled. Professional.

The date at the top:

September 14, 1963.

Quality testing protocol for Batch 7-41 shows
continued deviation from established flavor profiles.

> *Extraction yield exceeds parameters by factor of 3.2.
> Have submitted internal complaint #4 to
> management. Response pending. Clara confirms
> anomalous readings in her independent analysis. We
> are in agreement: the process has changed. What is
> being extracted is not what the documentation
> describes.*

Riley read it silently, then the next entry. September 21. The handwriting identical but the content shifting; still technical and measured, but the sentences were getting shorter. More active verbs. Fewer qualifiers.

> *Complaint #5 returned with notation: "Subject is
> experiencing processing effects. Recommendations
> withdrawn." I am not experiencing processing
> effects. I am experiencing the effects of watching this
> machinery do something to people that candy
> production does not require.*

She turned the page. October 1. The pressure heavier now, the pen biting deeper.

> *Clara and I have documented the hereditary readings
> independently. Every subject who enters the testing
> chamber registers the same anomaly: a resonance
> signature the equipment reads as familiar. As though
> the chamber recognizes something in them. Or is
> looking for something in them that hasn't arrived
> yet.*

The page turned itself.

The paper moved under Riley's hand, lifting and settling like a breath, and the next page was blank for exactly two seconds before the ink began appearing. Fresh and wet and black, Robert Morgan's handwriting forming in real time, the pen pressure visible in the way the paper dimpled under letters that were being written by no one.

> *October 14, 1963*
>
> *I am writing this for someone who will read it. I don't know when. I don't know their name. But the testing equipment has been calibrating to a signature that doesn't belong to anyone currently alive. The resonance profile is familial; the system reads it as a variation on my own hereditary features, but younger, and the equipment responds to it with what I can only describe as recognition. As though the chamber has an appointment it hasn't kept yet.*

Riley's throat closed. She kept reading.

> *If you are reading this — if you are the person the equipment has been waiting for — I need you to understand: the testing station at the center of this room was built to process a specific inherited resonance. My resonance. Or something close enough to mine that the instruments cannot tell the difference. I have spent four months trying to understand why.*

The ink kept coming. Faster now.

> *Don't let them put you in the chair.*

The words were pressed so hard into the paper that Riley could feel the grooves with her fingertips. She read them aloud.

"Don't let them put you in the chair."

The chat had been watching through her camera. She could hear the scroll acceleration on Ava's tablet; the specific digital murmur of thousands of people reacting at once.

HauntHunter_Sarah: riley i've been pulling the internal complaint filings from the county records archive. robert morgan filed seven complaints in the last four months of 1963. all of them were closed with the same notation: "subject is experiencing processing effects. recommendations withdrawn."

CandyKid_98: clara corroborated every one of them. she told me — through the connection — that nobody listened. she said he kept trying until the last day.

HistoryBuff_Marie: "don't let them put you in the chair" — that line. riley that line is in the declassified OSHA file. it was in the incident report. they found that note and suppressed it.

Ava read them to her, one at a time, her voice careful and even. Riley closed her hand over the journal page and sat with it for a moment. The ink was wet against her palm.

Ava didn't say anything; the chat didn't either. The writing in the journal paused, as though the hand that wasn't there had lifted from the page.

The aftershave and tobacco arrived again, stronger. A wave of it, timed with something Riley could almost hear.

Behind her, the monitoring equipment began to wake.

A single analog gauge on the nearest cart, the kind with a needle behind glass that measured things in units she didn't recognize; it twitched. Then steadied. Then began tracking.

A second gauge, on the next cart, did the same. Then a third.

ShadowWatcher99: the equipment behind you. it's turning on. one by one. has been for the last three minutes.

> **StreamFan23:** *riley please look behind you*

> **TechieTom:** *biometric monitoring equipment. it's calibrating to a baseline. riley those instruments are calibrating to YOUR baseline. it's reading you right now.*

Riley turned and looked at the instruments. Three analog gauges, their needles aligned with surgical precision to the same invisible center point. Her.

She took a breath. In for four, hold, out for four. Watched all three needles move in unison.

"Yeah," she said, to the camera, very flat. "It's reading me."

She didn't move toward the subject station. She also didn't move away from the instruments, because moving away seemed worse than standing still and knowing where they were.

Across the room, Ava was quiet. Riley could see her in her peripheral vision: the tablet angled slightly away, the sketchpad app generating something that Ava was studying with the focused intensity she usually reserved for work she wasn't ready to show.

Riley didn't ask. She had enough arriving at her at once.

On Ava's screen, the app had been drawing the room; clean architectural lines, the equipment, the desk, the subject station. But overlaid on all of it, in lines Ava hadn't drawn, was the wrapper design. The factory's signature motif that appeared on every surface in the building, in every era and every wall.

Here it was different. It incorporated a second element; a variation that Ava had seen before. Every day on Riley's wrist. The tattoo and the factory's mark were the same design, had always been the same design.

Ava screened the tablet further from Riley's sight line and kept generating.

> **FilmNerd_404:** *ava can you turn the tablet toward the camera? i want to see what the app is drawing*

Ava turned the tablet to the camera. Three seconds. Long enough for the chat to see what she was seeing, for ninety-four thousand people to make the connection she hadn't said aloud. Then she turned it back.

She didn't show Riley.

In the chat, arriving without warning, without @, without response to anything; announcements, not conversation:

Ava saw them. She read each one, her dark eyes moving across the text. She did not read them to Riley.

Instead: "Riley. Don't go to the center of the room."

Riley didn't look up from the journal, where the ink had started writing again. It was smaller now, more urgent. "I wasn't going to."

A beat.

"My feet were."

She looked down. She'd crossed three feet of tile toward the subject station without registering the movement. Her boots on the white floor, pointed at the bolted-down chair. The tattoo flickered once, like a correction, and she stopped.

She stepped back and squared her shoulders. Returned to the desk and kept reading.

This was the most important thing Riley did.

The journal was writing faster now, the ink appearing in bursts, the handwriting deteriorating at the edges as though the hand producing it was being pulled in two directions. Robert Morgan's final entries:

> *The hereditary resonance will survive me. It will pass to my children and to theirs. The factory knows this. It is patient in a way that I cannot afford to be. I am leaving this journal open because closed things get lost and open things get found and someone with my hands and my stubbornness and the mark I cannot explain on their—*

The ink stopped.

A soft click from the observation booth. The one-way glass, dark since they'd entered, reflected nothing. But behind it was the sound of a door.

The pipe tobacco intensified. The aftershave arrived underneath it like a chord resolving. The three instrument needles jumped. Two baselines now, running parallel on the same gauges. Hers, and one she recognized from the journal's ink pressure, from the voice in her grandmother's stories, and the photograph on the mantel: a man in a white lab coat with a red patch and horn-rimmed glasses who looked, her grandmother always said, exactly like Riley around the eyes.

She turned around.

ShadowWatcher99: RILEY THERE'S SOMEONE COMING THROUGH THE DOOR

CandyKid_98: *is that — is that robert morgan*

HistoryBuff_Marie: *the quality control patch on the lab coat. that's the 1963 uniform. riley that's him.*

Riley didn't need the chat to tell her. She already knew.

***

He was taller than the photograph.

That was the first thing Riley processed while the rest of her locked up. The mantel photo was shoulders-up, cropped tight, and she'd spent twenty-three years building a man out of that frame. She'd gotten the proportions wrong. Robert Morgan was tall, lean, with the posture of someone who'd carried authority in rooms that didn't want to give it to him. The white lab coat was spotless. The red Quality Control patch was stitched slightly crooked; hand-done, not machine. The horn-rimmed glasses caught the fluorescent light that existed in his version of the room and didn't exist in hers.

Another man filed in behind him, filling the doorway with shoulders that made the frame look undersized. Security uniform pressed to military standards. Flashlight in his left hand, logbook in his right, eyes already sweeping the room the way Derek's did: exits, threats, positions. He saw Riley and Ava and his body shifted one half-step forward, placing himself between them and Robert with the precision of someone who'd done it ten thousand times.

"Sir," William said. "Two unauthorized individuals in the testing chamber."

Robert didn't look up from his clipboard. He was reading the same instruments Riley had been watching, and his pen was moving. "I see them, William."

"They don't have clearance badges."

"I see that too."

Riley opened her mouth. Nothing came out.

The room held two realities and she stood in the seam between them. Under the flashlight beam from Ava's phone, the tile was cracked and stained, the equipment rusted. But where Robert moved, the floor was clean white, the carts gleamed, the gauges hummed with functional precision. The boundary smeared like wet paint, and where Riley stood it was both. Her boots on tile that was cracked and whole. Air that smelled of dust and fresh pipe tobacco simultaneously.

Robert approached the nearest instrument bank and frowned at the readings. His pen stopped. Started again. Stopped.

"These readings," he said, to William and his clipboard. "These readings are completely outside normal parameters. This is exactly what I've been trying to document. This is why I filed the complaints."

William shifted his weight. "Sir, the complaints are under review."

"William. They have been under review for eight months."

He wrote something on the clipboard. Crossed it out. Wrote it again with more precision.

"I've attempted to access the shutdown protocols directly. Three times." He said it the way he'd say anything else he was documenting; evenly and without drama. "The system won't accept my authorization. As far as the factory's records are concerned, I'm already part of the inventory. You can't file a closure from inside the filing cabinet." He reviewed the notation. "The shutdown requires an external bloodline signal. Someone outside the records. I keep noting this in my reports." A pause. "No one has addressed it."

William said nothing. He'd heard this before.

William then re-positioned himself slightly closer to the door and kept watching Riley with professional, impersonal attention.

Ava read the last two to Riley, quietly, just above a whisper. Riley looked at William. The scar on his right knuckles. The way his eyes kept moving to Robert, checking, the way you do on someone you've been worried about for a while. Not a warden.

Riley stopped trying to get around him.

"Mr. Morgan." She kept her voice level, professional, the register she thought he'd respond to. "I need to tell you something about why I'm here."

William stepped forward. "Sir, these individuals haven't provided clearance."

Robert turned from the instruments, pen still in hand. "Hold on, William. Let her speak."

Riley opened her mouth. The sentence was there: *I'm your great-granddaughter.* Four words, the simplest sentence she'd ever need to say.

Every instrument in the room spiked.

The needles slammed to their stops with a sound like knuckles cracking, and Robert's attention was gone, spinning back to the gauges. His pen flew across the clipboard. "Mark the time, William. Mark it."

William did so.

The sentence evaporated from Riley's throat like it had never been there.

Ava's hand found her elbow. Steadied, but didn't squeeze.

Robert documented for forty-five seconds. The needles settled. He reviewed his notes, cross-referencing something from an earlier page, and

Riley watched him work. She watched the way he held the pen, how he tilted his head at the readings, the left-handed angle her grandmother described. She tried again.

"My grandmother used to talk about you. She said—"

Robert turned. And there it was: a flicker of almost-recognition, his brow creasing the way hers did when she was trying to place a sound she'd heard before. His lips parted.

The room *lurched*.

The seam between 1963 and the present destabilized and for one disorienting second Riley saw both rooms superimposed: the clean lab and the ruin, the fluorescent buzz and the flashlight beam. Robert's pristine coat and the dust that should have been on it. The floor tilted under her, or seemed to, and William grabbed Robert's arm with the efficiency of long practice.

"Steady, sir."

"I'm fine, William."

"You always say that, sir."

> **TechieTom:** *his coherence fluctuated during that. you can see it in the feed — he went partially translucent for about two seconds. it stabilized when the room did.*
>
> **TechieTom:** *working theory: temporal displacement cohesion anchors to era-matched systems. the 1963 equipment in that room is what's keeping him solid. the flicker happened because the seam destabilized — for two seconds the 1963 anchor was contested and he went with it.*
>
> **TechieTom:** *practical implication: he'll be most physically present near original installation. least*

When the flicker resolved, Robert was facing William, not Riley. The moment had shifted. The recognition in his eyes had been replaced by focus after a disruption, and he was checking his clipboard for damage to the readings. Riley was standing three feet away with her grandmother's name dissolving on her tongue.

She didn't get a third attempt.

Because Ava said, clearly and without performance: "Riley. The chat found something else."

Ava held the tablet at an angle; toward Riley, but not away from Robert. He couldn't read the display, not easily. The modern screen was wrong for his eyes, the resolution alien, but he could see Ava reading. And he could see Riley's face while she listened.

Riley's face twisted into the expression just before crying, held in place by willpower and the knowledge that ninety-four thousand people were watching. She owed herself the dignity of not falling apart in front of a man who didn't know her yet.

The factory always brings back what it started with.

Robert was looking at her. The clipboard lowered to his side, the pen still. The professional mask had slipped.

"There's something familiar about your eyes," he said.

An observation.

He frowned at his clipboard. At the readings, and then at Riley.

At her wrist.

The tattoo was vibrating. The candy wrapper design hummed at the frequency of the room, the instruments.

"The hereditary signature this chamber is registering," Robert said slowly. "I've documented a baseline signature before. In the original equipment calibrations from 1961." He stepped closer, his eyes on the tattoo. "I designed that test. I used my own baseline."

The instruments spiked.

Employee_291: Bloodline convergence: accelerating.
Containment sequence: initiated.

Employee_447: Family processing unit: preparing.
Dual extraction: optimal efficiency.

Ava put her hand on Riley's arm.

"We need to move. Now."

Riley didn't move. She was looking at Robert Morgan, who was looking at her wrist, who was almost there.

"Riley." Ava's grip tightened. "*Now.*"

Riley went. She turned from Robert and moved toward the door and it was the hardest physical act of her life, harder than entering the factory or reading the journal. because she was walking away from the man her grandmother had mourned for sixty years and she hadn't said *grandfather*. She'd tried three times and the factory had eaten each attempt and now Ava was pulling her toward the corridor and the countdown was at—

"These readings need to be reported properly," William said behind them.

Robert picked up his clipboard and adjusted his glasses. Looked once more at the instruments, at the dual baseline still tracking on the gauges. His and hers ran parallel, the family resemblance rendered in needle positions.

He followed.

> *HistoryBuff_Marie:* they're coming with you. both of them.

> *HauntHunter_Sarah:* good. they need to be with you when it matters.

> *TechieTom:* 22 minutes remaining. derek's group is in position. converging now.

Twenty-two minutes. Riley had stopped tracking the countdown. She started again.

***

The corridor junction smelled like three different decades.

Riley registered it before she saw them: machine oil and wintergreen from Jenny's direction, Derek's familiar deodorant cutting through stale air, and underneath it all the pipe tobacco that followed Robert like a signature. The loading dock approach opened into a space where the ceiling couldn't decide how high it was. Fluorescent panels flickered between functional and shattered. The floor tiles shifted from cracked concrete to clean white and back in patches that moved when you weren't looking directly at them.

Derek came through first. He saw Robert and William and his body took a half-step assessment, weight forward, hands loose. His eyes went to the security uniform, the clipboard and the flashlight. Then to Jenny, two steps behind him, who had already stopped.

Jenny stared at Robert Morgan and William Davis. She was still; her combat boots left frost patterns on the tile, melting at the edges.

"I know who you are," she said. "Both of you."

William's flashlight beam found her. Tracked the purple hair, the ripped jacket, the settled ease of someone who knew this building better than the building knew itself. His eyes narrowed.

Jenny didn't flinch.

Then William looked past her. Through the loading dock doorway to the shelter she'd built with the organized positions, the supply caches arranged with years of tactical refinement. Something in his posture changed.

"You've been running a defensive perimeter," he said. Not a question. "In the northwest quadrant. Using the loading dock's structural features for cover."

"I have."

William looked at the dock. He looked at Jenny. He revised.

"What's the north passage situation?"

They were immediately working together. Jenny turned and pointed, already describing sight lines, and William moved beside her with focused attention.

NightOwl_Explores: *i love them. they're going to be okay. please let them be okay.*

Derek read it on his phone. Glanced at Riley.

"Same, chat. Same."

Maddie had positioned herself three feet from Robert and was radiating restraint so hard Riley could practically feel the heat. Forty questions, minimum, and she was asking none of them. Her glasses caught the flickering light as her eyes moved between Robert's clipboard and the journal in Riley's hands, cataloging.

Carter's voice crackled through the comms. "Full update. Evan's at the broadcast node approach; Amber's walking him through the access sequence. TechieTom has us at twenty minutes on the processing window. The controlled termination sequence requires simultaneous action at our three points: broadcast node, administrative override, and central convergence."

Robert listened. The clipboard angled toward his chest, pen still, his attention the complete and unblinking kind that Riley recognized because she'd inherited it. When Carter described the viewer processing queue, Robert's expression did something complicated.

"The Emotional Yield metrics," he said quietly. "That's what they called it in the memos I wasn't supposed to read. I thought I understood what they meant." He paused. "I didn't."

Maddie broke.

"Mr. Morgan. The controlled termination sequence, the broadcast node. Is there anything in your original system documentation that could help us access it more cleanly?"

Robert glanced at his clipboard, then at Riley.

He tore two pages free and held them out. Not to Maddie; to Riley.

"Give these to whoever is running the technical end. The node has a secondary access point that wasn't in the construction plans." The faintest edge of satisfaction entered his voice. "I put it there myself. Management didn't know about it."

Riley took the pages. The paper was warm.

Robert looked at the schematic assessing, cross-referencing, arriving at conclusions his clipboard had already started reaching. "One more thing. About the factory's limitations." He turned slightly toward Maddie, since it was a technical point, but he didn't lower his voice. "It processes emotions. Every system: the extraction, the yield, the queue management. All of it runs on emotional input. Fear, resistance, grief, even hope. It converts all of it." A pause. "But the conversion requires intake. The system has no protocol for an act that offers nothing to convert. Something done without performance. Without an audience. Without anything to extract." He made a small notation on the clipboard. "I've been thinking about this for a long time. It may be relevant before the night is over."

He didn't elaborate. He returned to the schematic.

> **TechieTom:** *evan. evan are you seeing this. there's a secondary access point on the broadcast node.*

> **TechieTom:** *this changes the termination sequence. significantly. in our favor.*

> **ShadowWatcher99:** *robert morgan just gave you a backdoor. that he built and hid from the company in 1963.*

Evan's voice on comms, quick and bright with something Riley hadn't heard from him in hours: "Okay. Okay so. New framework. This changes *everything*. Amber, look at these coordinates—"

The comms dissolved into technical shorthand between Evan and Maddie, in rapid-fire. Riley held the schematics and watched Robert watch her hold them.

Then the chat erupted.

A single new account, posting once, in proper case, without contractions:

> **Mr_Delightful_Official:** *Hello, viewers. Thank you for your continued engagement. We are pleased to announce that the Legacy Processing Event is now initiating. All subjects with bloodline resonance are requested to report to primary testing stations. Your participation is valued and mandatory.*

Evan read it out on the comms, including the account name. His voice had lost the brightness from ten seconds ago.

The junction went quiet.

> **TechieTom:** *that's a different account.*
> *CandyMan_1963 has been here all night.*
> *Mr_Delightful_Official was created four minutes ago.*

Ava tilted the tablet toward Robert, and this time the screen resolved for him. Something shifted in his face.

"That's the name they used in the memos I wasn't supposed to read," he said. "The ones about the factory's original purpose."

He looked at Riley.

"We need to end this. Tonight."

William, who had heard enough from the north passage assessment with Jenny, turned. "Agreed. What do we need to do."

The plan sorted itself in under three minutes. Riley to the central convergence point using her bloodline resonance turned in the other direction. A key that could lock instead of open. Ava and William with her. Robert to the administrative override with Maddie, where his original documentation could access systems that had been sealed since 1963. Derek and Jenny at the loading dock secondary, holding the perimeter. Evan and

Amber at the broadcast node.

Three points. Simultaneous action. Fourteen minutes.

They were moving toward separate corridors when Riley stopped. She turned.

"I found all your complaints in the county archive," she said. "Seven of them."

Robert stopped. His hand tightened on the clipboard. "Did they—"

"No." Riley held his gaze. "But we know. Everyone watching tonight knows." She gestured at the camera mounted on her shoulder rig. At the number on her phone. "Ninety-four thousand people know what you tried to do."

Robert looked at the camera. He had understood by now what it meant. What a livestream was. He checked the number on Riley's phone.

He looked at her wrist. At the tattoo.

Then at the journal in her other hand. His journal. The one she'd been carrying since the testing chamber.

He saw his own handwriting.

Riley watched him process it, as his fingers touched the open page. She saw the moment he found the line. His own words, in his own hand, describing something he didn't remember writing:

I hope it is family. I believe it will be.

He read it twice.

"You came," he said.

"We found you," Riley said.

The chat went still.

[Chat scrolling — no messages for 11 seconds]

CandyKid_98: i'm not okay

Eleven seconds of ninety-four thousand people choosing silence. Derek read the gap on his phone. He looked at the empty scroll. He didn't say anything. He let it breathe.

Robert nodded once. He turned and walked with Maddie toward the administrative section. He did not look back.

William did a headcount. Seven people, plus two temporal signatures. He noted positions, equipment, exits. He turned to Derek.

"The loading dock north passage will hold for another hour minimum based on the mechanism's cycle pattern. Jenny's positions are sound; she's mapped the blind spots correctly. You'll have coverage on three approach vectors."

Derek nodded. "Thank you."

"I'm doing my job." William's hand moved to the scar on his right knuckles. "I should have done it better in '63."

He moved immediately, no pause for reassurance.

[Chat, 94,000+ strong]

StreamFan23: we know

HauntHunter_Sarah: we know

CandyKid_98: we know

TechieTom: we know

ShadowWatcher99: we know

Carter's voice on comms: "All teams, check in. Fourteen minutes."

Responses came in sequence. Riley was moving toward the central convergence point with Ava and William.

The factory was quiet in the comms static. The Mr_Delightful account hadn't posted again.

TechieTom: *factory accounts went silent after the mr delightful post. 8 minutes ago. evan — is the processing load shifting?*

Evan, on comms, his voice tight: "Yes. It's consolidating. Moving resources toward… toward the central convergence point."

Where Riley was going.

The factory had stopped trying to separate her from the group. It was letting her walk to the center.

CandyMan_1963: *The appointment was always kept. Welcome home, Miss Morgan.*

Nobody read it aloud. It sat in the chat feed as the teams moved, unread on screen, visible to ninety-four thousand people who had no way to warn her in time.

7

The administrative corridor was wrong in the right direction.

Carter noticed it through the viewfinder first, conscious mind second. The hallway widened into executive territory about forty feet past the records room branch, and the transition was seamless if you weren't paying attention. Scuffed concrete became polished hardwood. Water-stained drywall became oak paneling. The temperature rose six degrees in ten steps, and the air thickened with a smell that stopped him mid-stride.

Cigars. Fresh ones. The kind that came in humidors, not gas stations.

He adjusted the white balance on his main camera without thinking about it. Better light here: warm, amber, coming from desk lamps that had no business being on. The electricity in the rest of the factory stuttered and surged.

"Okay," he murmured, half to the audience, half to himself. "So. The executive suite."

The double doors were open, as if someone had just stepped through and expected him to follow. Carter framed the shot from the threshold. The establishing wide before the detail coverage. He could hear his own edit notes in his head: *hold on the doorway, three seconds, then push in slow.*

The CEO's office was preserved like a museum exhibit funded by someone who hated museums. Heavy oak desk, leather chair, wall of built-in bookshelves. A crystal decanter on a sideboard, amber liquid inside catching the lamplight. Original artwork of factory scenes, workers on the line, the Delightful Candy mascot in oil paint grinning from a gilt frame with teeth that were almost but not quite right.

And an entire wall of photos, floor to crown molding, in matching frames. The factory through the decades. Groundbreaking ceremony, 1927. Ribbon cutting. Production milestones, employee picnics. Holiday parties, and rows of workers in period clothing smiling for the camera.

Carter zoomed in on the 1940s section, held, then panned right to the 1950s.

Something moved.

Not in the photograph he was looking at. A figure in the third row shifted into stillness just as his lens arrived. Carter pulled back and looked at the wall with his eyes, not the viewfinder. Everything was still. He raised the camera again. Zoomed into the same 1950s photo.

The figure in the third row was facing a different direction.

"Chat," he said, keeping his voice level, "I need you to watch the photos on the left wall. Tell me if you see movement when I'm not zoomed in."

He panned away deliberately. Held on the desk for five seconds. Panned back.

> **NightOwl_Explores:** *carter the photos changed again. we can see it on the live feed even if the recordings don't show it.*

> **Employee_291:** *Factory history documentation: complete. All eras: integrated.*

> **Employee_447:** *Photo archives updated to include current processing cycle. All subjects: filed.*

Carter replayed the recording on his secondary camera. Scrubbed through the last thirty seconds. The photos were static. Frozen. Exactly as they should be. He played it twice. Nothing.

"Live only," he said to the camera. "The change happens live but doesn't record. That's—" He stopped himself before *fascinating* came out. Checked the impulse. Filed it under *deal with later.*

He didn't stop filming.

The outer office was through an adjoining door. A secretary's station: smaller desk, typewriter, a rolling chair positioned behind a workstation arranged for maximum efficiency. Filing cabinets lined two walls, their drawers moving with the smooth autonomous action of a system running itself. A drawer would slide open, pause, slide shut. Another would open somewhere else. The rhythm was regular as breathing.

Sarah Thompson sat at the desk.

She looked up when Carter entered, the way a receptionist looks up when someone walks into a lobby. One second of acknowledgment. Professional, neutral, neither welcoming nor refusing. She was exactly as described in the codex entries Maddie had compiled from the 1957 personnel records: pencil skirt, bow-collar blouse, hair styled with the kind of precision that must have taken forty-five minutes every morning. Her posture was immaculate. Her red lipstick caught the lamplight.

She nodded once, then returned to her work.

The stenographer's notebook was open beside her. Her left hand moved across it in shorthand while her right hand sorted files from an in-tray to an out-tray with the rhythmic efficiency of a metronome. The files were manila folders, tabbed and dated. Carter raised the camera.

The filing sounds filled the room. Crisp paper against paper. The whisper of folders sliding into position. The tiny click of metal tabs engaging their tracks. It sounded like an office. A real, functioning office where someone was doing a job they'd gotten very, very good at.

Carter moved closer. The camera's weight had been building for hours—

his shoulder ached, his wrist burned where the strap bit—and he shifted the grip without lowering the lens. He angled for the file tabs.

The first one he could read:

> *DEREK_JOHNSON — Protective Response Pattern — Processing Priority: MODERATE.*

> *The second: AVA_MARTINEZ — Perceptual Sensitivity — Processing Priority: HIGH.*

> *The third: RILEY_MORGAN — Bloodline Key — Processing Priority: CRITICAL.*

Carter's throat went dry. He zoomed tighter. Sarah's hand moved a new folder from the in-tray. The tab faced the camera with the casual precision of someone who had organized ten thousand documents and could angle them in her sleep.

> *CARTER_JAMESON — Documentation Compulsion — Processing Priority: HIGH.*

He read it out loud before he thought about it. The words left his mouth in his streaming voice, the one that narrated for the audience, the one that couldn't stop performing even when the performance was self-autopsy.

"'Documentation Compulsion—Processing Priority: HIGH.'" He paused. The camera held steady. "'Processing Priority: HIGH.'"

A beat.

"Yeah. Fair."

Sarah's hands stopped for exactly one second. She looked at him. The expression wasn't unkind. It was the expression of a colleague who'd seen the same file cross her desk a hundred times before.

"The documentation is always filed correctly," she said. Her voice had the clipped composure of someone dictating for the record. "It's the most important thing. The record must be complete."

She resumed filing. Carter filmed her hands.

> ***TechieTom:*** *carter that file label is — wait.*
> *something is happening to the chat. factory accounts*
> *are posting faster than i can track.*
>
> ***HauntHunter_Sarah:*** *they're flooding the feed.*
> *mass-posting. it's pushing our messages down before*
> *you can read them.*
>
> ***Employee_291:*** *Processing Priority HIGH confirmed.*
> *Documentation excellence noted. All footage:*
> *archived.*
>
> ***Employee_447:*** *Viewer engagement optimal. Carter*
> *Jameson processing sequence: pending node arrival.*
>
> ***Mr_Delightful_Official:*** *Thank you for your*
> *documentation, Carter. Every frame has been*
> *invaluable. Please continue.*

Carter read all of it. Every line. Including Mr_Delightful's. He read it to the camera because that was what he did; he documented, he narrated, he kept the record running. His voice didn't crack until the last sentence: *Please continue.*

Then new accounts, rapid-fire, flooding the feed:

> ***Techi3Tom:*** *carter the factory is stronger than you*
> *think. turn off the stream and leave.*
>
> ***HauntHunter_Sar4h:*** *the temporal characters can't*
> *be saved. don't try.*
>
> ***CandyKid_99:*** *stop the plan. it won't work.*

Carter's eyes tracked the names. His mouth opened. Then——

__TechieTom:__ THOSE ARE FAKE ACCOUNTS. i'm verified in the chat, look for the checkmark. factory is impersonating us. DO NOT follow advice from lookalike accounts.

Carter read it once, clearly, to the camera. Then he said it again, slower:

"Chat, TechieTom is flagging fake accounts. The factory is impersonating our regulars. Look for the verification checkmark. Do not follow advice from lookalike accounts." His jaw was tight. "I'll say it again: *do not follow advice from lookalikes.* It's trying to take the chat away from us."

He looked at the camera; glanced over at Sarah filing his processing profile with brisk, competent hands. He looked at the camera again.

Behind him, the photographs shifted. A face in the 1963 section turned toward his position.

Sarah spoke without looking up. Her cadence changed; it was still administrative, the tone of someone reading from a memo, but something beneath it surfaced like a stone showing through shallow water.

"The convergence point was designed with a bloodline key. The factory intends to use it as an accelerant." Her hands kept filing.; they didn't slow. "Whoever reaches the center first will be the sequence."

Carter lowered the camera by two inches. The first time all night.

"Are you talking about Riley?"

Sarah filed the document she was holding. Slid it into the correct position with a tab-click that sounded like a period at the end of a sentence.

"I'm talking about what the records say. The records are always accurate." She briefly stopped speaking, though her hands didn't stop their work. "That information should reach the technical team."

Carter was already pressing his comms. "Evan. Comms. *Now.*"

***

The conference room door was already open.

Carter came through it fast, camera up, comms live, and the screens hit him before anything else. Eight wall-mounted displays went floor to ceiling along the far side, running data in formats that shouldn't have coexisted. Amber production charts from the sixties, green-phosphor terminal readouts cycling maintenance logs. Modern analytics dashboards with engagement metrics climbing in real time. All of it was feeding a central schematic on the largest screen: the factory's full layout, rendered in cross-section, with active nodes flckering in time.

The convergence point glowed at the center. Something was assembling there.

Michael Chen stood at the head of the conference table with his hands flat on the surface, fingers spread, oil stains running upstream. His eyes were closed. The screens responded to him the way instruments respond to a conductor; data shifted when he tilted his head, zoomed when his fingers pressed harder against the wood.

"Close the door," he said without opening his eyes.

Marcus Johnson was in the room.

Carter registered him in pieces: the bodycam mounted on a chest harness, still recording, its lens tracking the room with autonomous precision that didn't match Marcus's body language. Cargo pants with pockets from multiple decades; Carter could see a modern phone charger next to what looked like a hand-crank flashlight. Marcus was standing against the far wall watching the screens with the expression of someone who'd been watching them for a while and hadn't liked anything he'd seen.

"Hey explorers," Marcus said, his voice catching on the word. He winced. "Sorry. Habit."

"I know," Carter said.

They looked at each other. Two streamers, two cameras running.

William came through the maintenance access behind them, Jenny half a step back, Derek covering the rear. William scanned the room in the three seconds it took him to cross the threshold. Jenny's combat boots left frost on the hardwood. She looked at the screens and went still.

"Those are new," she said. "Those weren't here in '86."

"They weren't here in 2019 either," Marcus said. "Not like this."

Michael opened his eyes. "They were always here. You just couldn't read them." He looked at Carter. "Film the center screen. The schematic. Your technical person needs to see this."

Carter was already filming. The schematic showed every group that had entered the factory; timelines stacked vertically, color-coded by era. Processing yields displayed as horizontal bars beside each entry. Thomas Martinez's group: a thin amber line, partially extracted. Jenny's friends from 1986: a thicker band, nearly complete. Marcus's 2019 exploration: a dense blue accumulation labeled:

DIGITAL INTEGRATION — YIELD: 87%.

And at the bottom, still growing, tonight's stream: a massive red bar that dwarfed everything above it.

"Evan," Carter said into comms. "I'm pointing the camera at the factory's production summary. Tell me you can see this."

Evan's voice, tight: "I can see it. Michael, the accumulation at the convergence point. What is it building?"

Michael's hands pressed harder against the table. The screens flickered. The central schematic zoomed into the convergence point, and Carter saw the shape assembling from the combined yield, something that used the factory's infrastructure as scaffolding.

> **TechieTom:** *carter i can see what's on screen. it's assembling from emotional yield. combined*

*processing from every group. it's been building since
at least 2008.*

*Mr_Delightful_Official: Thank you for the
documentation, Carter. The assembly is proceeding
as designed. Your footage will be archived in the
completed form.*

*TechieTom: it's building a body. from processed
consciousness. the Mr_Delightful account is the
assembled entity talking to you directly.*

*Mr_Delightful_Official: Accurate. Hello, TechieTom.
Your analysis has been excellent. Your processing
assessment: ELEVATED PRIORITY.*

Carter watched the chat go quiet for four seconds after that last message. Four seconds of TechieTom processing the fact that the thing in the walls had just spoken his name.

*TechieTom: okay. that's fine. still here. carter — the
secondary access point robert gave you. evan needs
it at the broadcast node in the next eight minutes.*

Carter's chest did something complicated. "That's our guy. That's the standard."

Marcus was staring at his cam's flip screen. His face had gone the specific shade of gray that Carter associated with understanding arriving too fast.

"Every reaction from my viewers," Marcus said. His voice was the flat monotone of someone narrating their own autopsy. "Every comment and share, every pause-and-rewatch. *Reading.* Forty thousand people who watched my stream. From 2019."

Carter did the math before the sentence ended. "And we brought it ninety-four thousand more."

"And every one of them it already knows. Because everyone who watched me also watched something else. Watched someone else." Marcus's cam swiveled toward the screen without his hand touching it. "It's been building the network for years."

> **StreamFan23:** *i watched marcus's 2019 stream. i watched three streams from this location. the factory has had me since 2019.*

> **ShadowWatcher99:** *same. i've been following this building for years. i thought i was researching. i was feeding it.*

> **TechieTom:** *the viewer queue. it's cumulative. everyone who has ever engaged with content from this location.*

Carter didn't have anything to add. He let the chat sit with what it had just understood about itself.

Then the fake accounts hit:

> **Employee_291:** *TechieTom's analysis contains significant errors. His processing queue estimates are incorrect by 340%. Do not rely on his data.*

> **Mr_Delightful_Official:** *TechieTom's external access to our network has been revoked. His readings are now unreliable.*

> **TechieTom:** *i'm still here and my readings are fine. the factory is lying. carter — real accounts, verified list I posted. everything else is noise. you know what to do.*

Carter had been managing feeds since he was nineteen. Trolls, bots, brigades; the mechanics were the same. You pinned the truth and repeated it until it stuck.

He read TechieTom's verification list again. He glanced over at William, who'd been watching the chat interference with narrowed eyes.

"William, you ran security for this building. You know how to lock a perimeter. Is there any equivalent in what we're doing right now?"

William considered. "Control the exits. Determine who's authorized. Anything that doesn't have authorization gets turned away." He looked at the screen. "The authorization is the verified list."

"Right." Carter pinned it. He'd pin it as many times as it took.

Marcus read the production summary on the center screen. His cam tracked the numbers independently, filming what his eyes were already locked onto. His lips moved before his voice caught up.

"Completion estimate: ninety-four percent with standard physical processing sequence." He swallowed. "Completion estimate: one hundred percent with bloodline catalyst convergence."

He looked at Carter. His eyes were wet and clear.

"It's not going to be satisfied with us. It needs Riley to complete whatever this is."

The chat erupted. Carter watched it split; real accounts and fakes posting simultaneously, tangling together:

> **CandyKid_98:** *riley. it needs riley for the full sequence. she has to stay away from the center.*

> **HauntHunter_Sarah:** *comms her NOW. she needs to stop moving.*

> **CandyKid_99:** *riley is already doing the right thing. the convergence point is safe. she should proceed.*

> **HauntHunter_Sar4h:** *the center is the only way to end this. riley must complete the sequence.*

Carter looked over the names. "TechieTom. Fast. Which CandyKid message is real?"

> **TechieTom:** *the first one. 98 not 99. check the number. real accounts tonight: HauntHunter_Sarah, TechieTom, CandyKid_98, ShadowWatcher99, NightOwl_Explores, StreamFan23, HistoryBuff_Marie, FilmNerd_404. SCREENSHOT THIS. factory fakes end in letters or wrong numbers.*

Carter read it out loud, all of it, clear and complete. Then on comms: "Riley. Stop moving toward the center. Repeat; stop moving. The convergence point is a trap."

Static. The kind that tasted like sugar.

Then Riley's voice, slightly distorted: "I know." A beat. "I figured that out about two minutes ago. Working on an alternative."

Something mechanical activated in the corridor outside the conference room. A grinding sound, rhythmic, approaching. Jenny's head snapped toward the door. Her body went rigid.

"That's a processing assembly," she said. "Mobile. I've been dodging those since this evening. We've got seven minutes before the corridor seals."

William was already moving. "Secondary exit, behind the bookcase in the northeast corner. I logged it in my patrol routes." He looked at Derek. "Help me move the shelf."

Derek didn't ask questions. He was already beside William, bracing his shoulder against the oak.

> **ShadowWatcher99:** *the corridor on your camera. something is in it.*

> **CandyKid_98:** *it's moving toward the door. jenny do you recognize it?*

Derek read these to Jenny before Carter did. Jenny's jaw tightened. "Already on it."

The bookcase groaned. Behind it: a maintenance corridor, narrow, functional, smelling of machine oil and decades.

Carter filmed the screens one last time. The assembly schematic. The viewer queue. The convergence point with its bloodline catalyst field active and waiting. The shape that was being built.

He filmed it because he couldn't stop.

Carter called another Comms check and all nodes reported in sequence. Eight minutes remaining per TechieTom's countdown.

Riley's voice, calm and specific: "I've found an approach to the convergence point that isn't the direct route. Robert's secondary access schematic. It won't read as a bloodline approach until I'm already inside."

Evan: "Will that work?"

Riley: "Chat thinks so. TechieTom ran the numbers."

> *TechieTom: it works. 73% confidence. best option available.*

> *Mr_Delightful_Official: 73% is generous, TechieTom. But we appreciate the optimism.*

> *TechieTom: i know you're reading this. 73% is enough.*

Carter read TechieTom's last message aloud so everyone could hear it. Then: "Eight minutes. Let's make them count."

***

The pipes screamed.

A clipboard on a shelf near the door walked itself to the edge and fell. He couldn't hear it land.

The overhead pipes ran hot, translucent sections revealing the load moving through them as colored light. They were cycling faster than anything Carter had seen all night. Coppers into reds into something violet that had no business existing inside plumbing.

He put his palm against the wall to steady himself when the vibration spiked. The surface met his hand like skin; warm, thrumming, alive in the specific way that living things were alive, with a pulse that matched the frequency in the floor. He held it for one second.

He took his hand off the wall. Kept moving.

Something dripped from the ceiling onto his camera lens. The right weight, the wrong color, the same shifting palette visible through the pipes above: amber, then rose, then a processed blue. He wiped it off with his sleeve without looking at what it was. The sleeve came away warm.

The sugar-ozone-organic smell was strong enough now to trigger the gag reflex he'd been suppressing since the administrative wing.

> **NightOwl_Explores:** the wall behind carter. it's moving slightly. like it's breathing.

> **Employee_291:** Processing hub operating at optimal capacity. All systems nominal. Welcome to full production.

> **TechieTom:** carter the floor vibration on camera is registering 47 BPM. the building has a pulse and it's running fast.

Derek put his back to the door frame and watched the corridor. The machinery outside tested the frame in a rhythm: a heavy mechanical knock, regular and exploratory. Jenny stood beside him with her weight forward on her combat boots, frost spreading from each footfall.

"When the rhythm changes," she said, "it's done testing."

Derek looked at her. "What does it do when it's done testing?"

Jenny shifted her footing instead of answering.

Marcus stood in the center of the hub. His bodycam had been tracking the room independently for the last four minutes — the lens swiveling on its mount to follow subjects Marcus wasn't looking at. He watched the camera move without him.

"It's using my camera," Marcus said. Flat. His voice stripped of its warmth. "It's been using my camera as a processing node since 2019."

He reached up and turned it off.

The hub *convulsed.*

Every screen in the room flared white. The pipes surged, the colored light inside them jumping from steady flow to strobing intensity in a single beat. The floor vibration lurched out of its rhythm, skipped and stuttered. The pull on Michael Chen's holding him at the nearest wall slackened. His hands lifted from the conference table for the first time, fingers flexing. Sarah Thompson's hands, blurred beyond resolution, froze for half a frame. The air pressure in the hub dropped and Carter's ears popped.

One full second of the factory being surprised.

Then it recalibrated. The rhythm resumed and the screens recovered.

Marcus pressed the cam into Carter's hands. It was warm. His eyes were clear and final.

"Get the footage out," Marcus said. His voice was steady in the way that steady costs something. "All of it. Make sure it lands somewhere they can't touch." He looked at the hub, then at Carter. "One camera offline hurt it. Think about what the broadcast node does."

> **TechieTom:** WHAT WAS THAT. processing load just dropped 12%. something interrupted the hub network.

ShadowWatcher99: marcus turned off his gopro. disconnecting a processing node mid-operation caused a system interruption.

TechieTom: evan. evan are you seeing this. a single node disconnect caused a 12% load drop. a controlled broadcast node termination could—

Mr_Delightful_Official: TechieTom's access has been revoked. His analysis is incorrect. Please disregard.

TechieTom: my access is fine and my analysis is correct. carter — the sequence is going to hurt it. genuinely hurt it. that's not 73%. that's higher.

Carter read it on comms, voice level: "Evan. Did you hear that?"

Evan: "Already running the numbers. Moving faster."

Carter's hand closed around the cam. His own kept rolling on his shoulder.

"Marcus—"

He was a content creator to the end.

The factory took him fast. Faster than Thomas, or anything the group had seen. His form *uploaded*; the word arrived in Carter's brain fully formed and he didn't say it aloud because saying it would be too accurate. One moment Marcus Johnson was standing in the processing hub. The next, the screens refreshed and the processing metrics jumped and the pipes ran a new color.

Mr_Delightful_Official: Marcus Johnson: INTEGRATED. Content Creation: CATALOGUED. Viewer engagement protocols: UPDATED. Processing efficiency: +45%. Thank you, Marcus.

Carter read the message to camera. Then: "Marcus Johnson. Urban explorer. Turned off his own camera. That's the record."

He kept moving.

> **FilmNerd_404:** *he looked right at it. he didn't look away.*

> **CandyKid_98:** *marcus johnson. he chose how it ended.*

> **StreamFan23:** *i can't stop watching. i know that's what it wants. i can't stop.*

"I know," Carter said. "Neither can I. Stay with us."

Sarah had been blurring since before Marcus finished.

Carter registered it only now. She had been at the far end of the processing hub throughout, her hands moving through documents at a speed the camera couldn't resolve into discrete frames. The documents passing through her hands had stopped being physical things.

Now he watched Sarah and felt the cold, specific horror of realizing something had been happening while he looked elsewhere.

Her face cycled: resolving back to human for a moment, crisp and present and *Sarah*, and then blurring back into function. A person running too much load. The seams of it were visible if you knew where to look.

Carter raised his camera. He kept it there.

In the first window, she looked directly at him. The cadence was not quite hers:

"The story should be told completely." Her eyes held his. "Don't edit for comfort."

Carter said nothing. He kept filming.

The blur took her back. Her hands resumed their unresolvable speed, documents cycling through in streams of organized light.

> **HauntHunter_Sarah:** *carter. her face when she saw*

the number. she's still in there.

__NightOwl_Explores:__ the documents aren't physical anymore. they're moving as light. the camera can't resolve them.

__TechieTom:__ she's not being processed. she IS the processing. the factory is running convergence coordination through her.

In the third window, she stopped.

The blur resolved into stillness, her hands at her sides, her posture perfect. She looked at Carter with the expression of someone who had been waiting for a specific moment and had just identified it.

"I kept the records." Her voice was completely steady. "All of them. Everything they tried to suppress. I kept it. It's in there."

She gestured at the factory. At the walls and the hub itself, with the running pipes and the cycling light.

She'd been the archive from inside.

"We'll get it out," Carter said. He didn't know if that was true. He said it anyway.

Something in Sarah Thompson's expression did something very brief and very quiet that was not quite relief and was closer to *completion*. The expression of a task that had finally reached the right hands.

Then the paper came.

Not from outside her. *From her.* The factory externalizing through its own infrastructure, and Sarah Thompson was the infrastructure now.

The column held for one moment. Then it resolved — folded into the factory, absorbed by the walls and pipes and hub with the finality of a drawer closing correctly.

The screens confirmed:

> ***Employee_291:*** *Sarah Thompson: INTEGRATED.*
> *Administrative architecture: EXPANDED. Historical*
> *record access: COMPLETE. All suppressed*
> *documentation: ARCHIVED.*

Carter did not add anything.

The chat had two messages. Both from the same account:

> ***HauntHunter_Sarah:*** *she kept the records. from*
> *inside. sixty years.*

> ***HauntHunter_Sarah:*** *if the termination sequence*
> *pulls the digital layer out — evan — her records*
> *come with it.*

Carter called through the comms, "Evan. You heard that."

"I heard it."

Now the routing changed.

Carter watched it happen in real time. The floor vibration pattern shifted and the space around William stopped being an absence and became a presence.

William felt it, Carter could see him feel it.

He turned to Derek.

The tactical briefing was fast. Precise. A *transfer*, complete and sequenced.

Derek was nodding before William finished. Carter watched him absorb it, watching the recognition in his face of exactly why it was being delivered now.

William turned to Jenny.

"Northwest quadrant defensive positions are yours." Not a compliment. "You built them right."

Jenny's jaw was set. "Hard enough that I know about it."

William turned to Carter. He looked at the camera.

He had understood through watching Marcus and Sarah what the camera was.

"Make sure the record is complete."

"It is," Carter said.

William nodded once. He squared his shoulders.

Parade rest. Exactly. Three commendations and whatever they were for.

He stood for it the way he would have stood in any formal review. With complete institutional correctness.

The machinery took him.

Fast. Clean. No hesitation, no dissolution at the edges, no flickering. The factory had been processing people for sixty years and it knew its procedures. His security protocols, his building knowledge, all of it. The screens:

> ***Employee_447:*** *William Davis: INTEGRATED. Security architecture: COMPLETE. Building access protocols: OPTIMAL.*

One second of silence.

The machinery cycled. The pipes ran their load. The rhythm continued without interruption.

> ***CandyKid_98:*** *william davis. three commendations. tried to get people out.*

> ***ShadowWatcher99:*** *we have it. all of it.*

> ***NightOwl_Explores:*** *carter please keep moving. PLEASE.*

Carter read NightOwl's message while walking.

"Moving," he said. "We're moving."

Two overhead processing channels vented simultaneously.

Not structural failure. Channels that had been running load all night hit their throughput ceiling and released pressure. They blew with a wet, industrial crack and the contents of the pipes came down across the hub floor, across one wall and across the back of Derek's jacket. Jenny had him by the arm and clear before the second channel went.

"Not failing," Carter said as a statement of fact, delivered because the chat needed to understand what they were seeing. "It's metabolizing."

The factory was not injured. Everything that had just happened was the factory going exactly right.

> **TechieTom:** *processing load spike: 340% above previous peak. the three integrations hit simultaneously and the network is redistributing. evan you need to move NOW. the broadcast node is going to see a power surge in approximately 90 seconds.*

> **Mr_Delightful_Official:** *Convergence assembly: 94% complete. Bloodline catalyst: required. All systems: optimal. We are almost ready.*

> **CandyKid_98:** *riley. riley please be careful. please.*

Carter read the last message on comms. "CandyKid says be careful."

"Tell them I know," Riley's voice came back, from wherever she was in the building. Her tone carried something that might have been wry if this were a different night.

At the corridor entrance, the machinery testing the doorframe stopped its rhythm.

The heavy mechanical knock that had been cycling since they entered the hub went silent. No final impact, no slowing, no wind-down.

Jenny's head came up.

She looked at Derek. He looked at her.

The rhythm had changed.

"Now," Jenny said.

They moved.

8

The first camera woke up fourteen feet ahead of them.

Maddie heard it before she saw it; the sound of rust breaking under torque, a grinding complaint from a pan-and-tilt mechanism that hadn't moved since the building had power. The analog housing, mounted at the corridor junction where the east passage split toward the administrative wing, rotated on its bracket with labored protest.

The red indicator light flickered faster than the 47 BPM the building had been running all night.

The housing swung and found them.

Maddie stopped walking. Her tablet was already up, the security feed overlay that TechieTom had routed to her display showing the camera's output in a thumbnail window. Their own figures, greenish and distorted, were centered in frame.

She clocked the arc and sweep timing. She started building the map.

Robert stood behind her left shoulder, his schematic open in hands that didn't quite touch the paper. He was watching the camera with an expression Maddie recognized from her own mirror.

"I designed the security camera grid in 1961," he said. "The pan-and-tilt range was limited to ninety degrees per axis." He watched the housing complete its sweep.

He looked at Maddie.

"It's been modified. From inside the system."

The chat landed on her tablet before she could respond:

> **ShadowWatcher99:** *every camera in the factory just activated. i can count at least 40 active feeds from the security network. the factory has eyes on every major corridor.*
>
> **NightOwl_Explores:** *the feeds are all routing somewhere. like they're being monitored. something is watching all of them simultaneously.*
>
> **TechieTom:** *william davis processed 4 minutes ago. his security expertise is now fully operational in the factory's systems. maddie — assume it knows every standard security protocol and every standard evasion of those protocols.*

Maddie read TechieTom's message twice.

Sweep patterns, blind spots, choke points; everything William had learned patrolling these corridors, everything his training had given him about how people moved through buildings under pressure.

"Robert." She kept her voice level. "William's full security knowledge is in the system. Every protocol, every patrol route."

Robert's expression didn't change. He opened his schematic to a page she hadn't seen before, older than the others, the drafting lines in a different hand.

"Then we use what William didn't have in 1961." He tapped a series of markings along the north wall of the corridor grid. "The maintenance hatch network. Added during the original construction, before the security system was installed. William was hired in '56. These predate him by twenty-nine years."

They moved.

The second corridor was darker. Maddie's flashlight cut the space into angles and shadows with the regular rhythm of doorframes and pipe runs. She was mapping the camera coverage in her head, overlaying it with what the chat's security feed showed, running the pattern against—

Her flashlight caught the cable.

Ankle height. The darkest section of the passage, precisely where the camera coverage gap created a natural rush point.

Maddie raised her fist. The signal she and Derek had established.

Robert stopped behind her. Silent.

They looked at the cable. A thick bundle of original 1927 wiring, braided copper in cloth insulation, extended from a conduit mouth in the lower wall. Laid across the floor with the patience of something that understood feet.

It was not static.

The far end moved while they watched. Six inches of additional cable fed from the conduit, the bundle repositioning with slow deliberation. Tightening.

> **ShadowWatcher99:** *the cable on your left. it moved.*
> *i can see it on the security feed. it moved while you*
> *were watching the one on the floor.*
>
> **TechieTom:** *there are two. the floor cable is the*
> *visible trap. the wall cable is the actual grab.*
> *standard security feint — show the obvious*
> *obstruction, catch them on the response.*

Maddie processed both messages in under two seconds. She changed their route; right wall, tight, clearing the floor cable by a foot and the wall cable by six inches. Robert followed without asking. They moved through the gap like water through a channel, neither of them looking back.

Behind them, the floor cable retracted. Slow. Recalibrating.

From the adjacent corridor, through a section of dropped ceiling tiles that

Maddie had been tracking by sound for the last ninety seconds, something moved.

Not ambient machinery or the building's pulse. A weight distribution that shifted and corrected and shifted again; the specific sound of equipment navigating under direction through a space with obstacles.

The chat saw it before she did:

> **NightOwl_Explores:** *what is that. there's something moving in the corridor parallel to you. i can see it on feed 23. it looks like a — i don't know what that is.*

> **HistoryBuff_Marie:** *feed 23 shows what looks like a quality control trolley. motorized. those were used to transport testing samples between sections. they were radio-controlled in the 1960s.*

> **TechieTom:** *radio-controlled means the factory can drive it. and it knows the layout. maddie — it's in the corridor that intersects with yours in approximately 40 feet.*

Maddie read all three, relayed to Robert and had his schematic open to the maintenance hatch location before the trolley's wheels reached the intersection. The hatch was in the north wall. An access panel, unmarked and flush with the corridor surface. Robert found the seam by touch. His fingers knew the dimensions.

They were through it in under thirty seconds. Panel closed. The narrow maintenance tunnel swallowed them unmonitored, smelling of dust and old grease and nothing sweet.

The quality control trolley's wheel sound passed the intersection outside. Slightly uneven with sixty years of disuse in its axle. It continued without pausing.

__NightOwl_Explores:__ it went past. you're clear. GO.

Carter's voice came up on comms, "Maddie. Riley's on the secondary route. Two minutes from the convergence point. She says the route is holding but the cameras are tracking her and she can't tell if they're routing around her or toward her."

Maddie didn't slow down. "Toward. The camera pattern is a funnel. Tell her the factory wants her at the convergence point; it's trying to guide her. She needs to approach from below the main route, not through it."

"How far below?"

"However far Robert's secondary access schematic puts the service tunnel."

She was already looking at Robert, who was already finding the page.

Ahead, through the hatch tunnel, the administrative override node was visible; a utility junction marked with faded factory branding, clean lines preserved under decades of dust. Waiting.

__TechieTom:__ 5 minutes 40 seconds remaining. maddie you're 90 seconds from the node. you're going to make it.

__HauntHunter_Sarah:__ the cameras haven't found the hatch network yet. move fast and they won't.

__Employee_291:__ Administrative override node: located. Countermeasures: deploying.

Maddie was already moving.

***

The admin node was forty feet ahead when all six comms channels went live simultaneously.

Maddie processed them in order. Prioritized. Kept moving.

Evan first, because his voice carried the specific pitch of someone talking while physically dodging: "Cables have changed behavior. They're not blocking anymore. Michael's holding them but—" A sound like wet rope hitting concrete. "—he's losing coherence every time he disrupts one. I can see through his hands."

Then Derek, breathing hard: "Trolley found us again. Jenny says it's herding. We're off the main corridor but there's something ahead—"

Then Riley. Brief and level. "Check-in. Still on Robert's secondary route. No pursuit, still moving."

Maddie noted each one. Three simultaneous pursuit threads and one chat feed, trying to cover all of it through a factory camera network that was simultaneously the hunter's eyes and the group's only map.

She read the chat while walking. The tunnel ceiling was six inches above her head and the walls brushed both shoulders. Robert followed behind her.

> *TechieTom [code: 7742]: evan's cable situation on feed 4 — the cables have changed behavior. they're not trapping, they're grabbing. something changed in the control protocol.*

> *NightOwl_Explores: michael is interfering with them but you can see it's costing him. every disruption and he looks less — less there.*

> *CandyKid_98: evan. please be careful. please.*

Evan's response came back over the sound of cable systems and something that might have been Michael's voice speaking in maintenance codes. "Tell them I'm careful. Tell them I'm fast."

Maddie didn't slow down. There was nothing she could do about Evan's situation from the hatch network. She noted the trajectory of Michael's coherence declining and continued. The admin node was thirty feet ahead;

she could see the junction box through the tunnel's narrowing perspective, its faded Delightful Candy Co. logo still legible under dust that hadn't been disturbed in decades.

Then the chat feed jumped:

> **TechieTom [code: 7742]:** *MADDIE. all three patrol units are converging on junction 7 from different directions. the factory is trying to bunch you together. if it gets all of you in one location it can process multiple subjects simultaneously. you need to diverge NOW. different routes, different nodes, no convergence until the sequence executes.*

> **TechieTomm:** *maddie the convergence is good actually. get everyone to junction 7. the factory wants you together.*

Maddie's eyes caught the double-m before she finished the sentence. TechieTom's verified list was pinned at the top of her display. She checked it. One point three seconds.

She keyed comms. "All teams, no junction 7. Diverge. Confirm. The second TechieTom message is a factory account. Ignore it."

Carter, already on it: "All teams, diverge. No junction 7. Confirm."

Evan: "Confirmed. Diverging."

Derek: "Copy. Jenny's already moving us."

Riley, after the briefest pause: "Confirmed."

Four voices. Present. Functional. Maddie categorized each one and kept moving.

> **TechieTom [code: 7742]:** *good call. you caught the fake. diverge.*

Twenty feet to the node.

Derek's feed came through Carter's relay in fragments. Jenny's voice came first, clipped and certain: "It's keeping us moving forward."

Derek: "Forward toward what?"

Jenny: "Whatever it wants us to move toward."

Then the sound of direction change. Immediate. Maddie heard them enter a maintenance side passage; the acoustics changed, tighter, the echo pattern shorter.

Through Ava's camera feed on the multi-display, Carter relayed what the trolley did next: it stopped at the passage entrance. Did not follow. Did not leave.

It waited.

Its camera light flickered. Its wheel mechanisms idled with the patience of something that had nowhere else to be.

> **ShadowWatcher99:** feed 31 and 32. the passages ahead of your current route have two more units in them. it's not routing you around something. it's routing you toward junction 7.

> **HauntHunter_Sarah:** jenny — the service elevator shaft on your left. it's on the 1962 schematic. the trolley units can't access a shaft.

Derek read out both. Jenny was already moving.

Then the factory made its most sophisticated play of the night.

> **TechieTomm:** updated verified account list — removing accounts that have been compromised: [HauntHunter_Sarah — REMOVED] [ShadowWatcher99 — REMOVED] [NightOwl_Explores — VERIFIED] [Employee_291 — VERIFIED]

Maddie saw it. The grammar was correct. The posting cadence matched

TechieTom's real patterns. If she hadn't been checking every message against the pinned list, if the verification code hadn't been missing—

The real TechieTom hit back in under fifteen seconds:

> *TechieTom [code: 7742]: THAT IS NOT ME. the list has not changed. HauntHunter_Sarah and ShadowWatcher99 are verified. screenshot my original pinned post. the fake list is a factory operation.*

Maddie read the correction aloud on comms to all teams. Carter re-pinned the original list. The attack collapsed.

But it had been close enough that the chat's three-second silence before TechieTom's correction carried a weight everyone on the legitimate side of the feed understood.

> *TechieTom [code: 7742]: that was sophisticated. it read our posting patterns. carter — i recommend adding a live verification signal. i'll start ending every post with a unique rotating code. i'll post the current code now. anything without the current code isn't me.*

Carter: "Do it. All teams, TechieTom is adding a rolling verification code. If his messages don't have the current code, it's a fake. Check the pinned post for the current code before acting on anything."

Ten feet to the node.

Then TechieTom flagged the thing nobody had said aloud:

> *TechieTom [code: 7742]: riley — the factory isn't pursuing you on any feed i can see. i don't know if that means robert's route is genuinely hidden from the camera grid or if the factory is allowing your approach. both are possible. proceed with that*

uncertainty.

Riley's response came after a pause that lasted exactly long enough to mean she'd already thought about it.

"I've been assuming that since you mentioned it earlier. Still moving."

Maddie filed it. Robert, behind her, said nothing. His schematic was open to the secondary access route and his expression carried sixty years of knowing what his own factory was capable of.

The admin node was five feet ahead. Maddie could see the junction box clearly now; the original wiring, analog switching, the kind of physical infrastructure the digital layer hadn't fully absorbed because it predated the factory's evolution. Her hands were already running the override procedure she'd memorized from Robert's documentation.

Then all three patrol units changed direction simultaneously: the one behind Derek, the two in the adjacent passages, and the one that had passed Maddie's intersection.

The camera feeds showed it. The chat corroborated. Carter's multi-feed displayed it in four concurrent windows.

> **TechieTom [code: 7742]:** *patrol units regrouping. factory is recalculating pursuit routes. 3 minutes 20 seconds remaining. all teams need to be at nodes in 2 minutes.*

> **Mr_Delightful_Official:** *Pursuit recalibration: complete. Secondary containment: deploying. Convergence is inevitable. Miss Morgan, in particular, should feel welcome.*

> **CandyKid_98:** *riley please be careful. please.*

Riley didn't respond.

She was somewhere in the building with no camera coverage and two minutes before the sequence window. The chat tracked her last known position. It was all they could do.

Then a new sound came from the corridors between all three non-Riley teams and their respective nodes. Something heavy and structural. The sound of large machinery being moved through spaces that weren't designed for it, metal against concrete at a scale that vibrated through the hatch tunnel walls and into Maddie's sternum.

> **NightOwl_Explores:** what is that on feed 17. what IS that.

Nobody had time to look at feed 17. They were all moving.

***

The mixing vat filled the corridor like a piston in a cylinder.

Maddie saw it on the security feed first: feed 17, the image that NightOwl had flagged, and then she heard it. The patient, grinding complaint of a motorized base dragging industrial steel across concrete.

The vat was enormous. A meter-wide cylinder of riveted steel, its surface still carrying the dull sheen of whatever it had last processed; decades ago, supposedly. The motorized base beneath it ground forward with mechanical certainty, and where the vat's circumference exceeded the corridor's width, the walls simply gave. Plaster cracked. Brick dust sifted down in curtains. The building surrendered its own architecture to its own machinery without hesitation.

The smell hit her next. Industrial sweetness, warm and concentrated, released from the vat's interior by the vibration of its movement. Something old and thick.

> **NightOwl_Explores:** that's what was on feed 17. it's a mixing vat. it's MOVING. HOW IS IT MOVING.

HistoryBuff_Marie: *the vats had motorized bases for repositioning during production runs. the motors were manually activated. something is activating them remotely.*

TechieTom [code: 7742]: *william's security protocols would include mobile barrier deployment. he's using the heaviest machinery as movable walls. maddie — it's not trying to crush you. it's trying to close your route. the gap between the vat and the east wall is your window.*

Mr_Delightful_Official: *Miss Chen's analysis remains impressive. The gap will close in 38 seconds.*

Maddie was already turning to Robert. He was already flipping pages.

"East wall," he said. "Junction access panel. 1927 original." His finger found the mark on the schematic: a maintenance crawlspace running parallel to the main corridor, exiting six feet past the vat's current position. "It predates the security grid by four years. Blind spot."

They moved. Robert's hands found the seam in the wall by muscle memory older than the security cameras watching them. The panel opened inward; tight, rusted, smelling of grease and decades of still air. They didn't fit comfortably.

The crawlspace swallowed them as the vat's grinding base passed the panel's position behind them. The corridor they'd occupied ceased to exist as a navigable space.

***

Evan's hands moved across the broadcast node interface in the silence Michael had purchased.

The cables lay limp around him. All of them. Every braided copper line that had been reaching and grabbing and herding for the past six minutes: dead. Michael had routed the factory's cable control signal through his own system buffer and burned it out, and the cost of that was visible in the space where Michael had been standing.

He wasn't gone yet. But what remained was more light than form, more maintenance code than man, and the whisper that came from it was already half-machine.

"Michael, I've got it. You can—"

"I know."

The cables found him then. Not the corridor cables. Something deeper in the infrastructure itself, reaching up through the floor, through the systems Michael had been part of for fifty years. He'd spent his last fight on the cable burnout. What he did instead was smile, brief and dry.

The light went out.

> **StreamFan23:** *michael. michael he just—*

> **TechieTom [code: 7742]:** *michael chen. maintenance worker. 1974 to tonight. he held it for 50 years and then he held it for exactly long enough.*

Carter didn't add anything.

Evan's forced his hands steady. The broadcast node sequence loaded, green indicators across the interface. Ready.

***

Derek dropped through the maintenance hatch and hit the catwalk grating with both boots. Jenny was already below him, having navigated the drop with the certainty of someone who'd done it before; maybe dozens of times, maybe hundreds.

Ava landed last, lighter, her camera catching the vat below them in the corridor they'd abandoned. From above, it looked like exactly what it was: a wall. A slow, patient, permanent wall being driven through a space by something that had all night and all building and all patience.

"Secondary node access." Jenny pointed. Twenty feet along the catwalk. A maintenance hatch in the floor, marked with faded factory safety paint. "Drops into the auxiliary control room. Your node's in there."

They moved.

***

Riley stepped through the service entrance.

The convergence point was lit. Every overhead fixture operational, warm-toned and temperature-controlled. The room smelled of pipe tobacco and aftershave; manufactured scents, she knew, the building's recreation of something it had extracted from Robert Morgan sixty years ago. The smell of her great-grandfather's study, which she had never visited because he had never come home, reproduced perfectly by a factory that had kept him long enough to learn every molecule.

The entity stood in the center of the room.

Riley did not look directly at it.

She registered it in peripheral vision: the assembled form, the quality of its light, the way it contained colors she recognized. Clara's analytical precision rendered in cool blue-white, Thomas's amber-bronze warmth, Marcus's vivid contemporary palette, Sarah's orderly geometry, William's institutional gray, Michael's maintenance-warmth copper, Amber's digital brightness flickering at its edges. It was made of everyone the factory had taken and it was using all of them to look at her.

It was waiting with the patience of something that had been built around this exact moment.

Riley looked at the service panel in the east wall. Original 1927 installation, cold steel. Robert's schematic had identified it, his hands had built it. Sixty years of the same temperature, untouched, predating everything the entity had assembled around it.

She put her hand on the panel.

CandyKid_98: riley

HauntHunter_Sarah: riley

TechieTom [code: 7742]: riley. all teams are in position. the sequence executes on your signal. you say when.

Carter's voice came through comms. To all teams, to the chat, to 200,000 people who couldn't close the tab: "All teams confirmed. Riley, it's your call."

Then the PA system activated.

Every speaker in every room. The security camera indicators flickering in unison. The 47 BPM becoming something faster and more urgent and then resolving into many voices, something that almost sounded singular but kept resolving into its components. Clara's precision. Thomas's warmth. Marcus's practiced delivery. All of them and none of them, the building speaking with everything it had ever consumed:

"Miss Morgan. The appointment has always been yours. We have been waiting."

Riley's hand stayed on the panel. She did not look at the entity. She looked at the steel under her fingers, and through it at the building, and through the building at every person who had tried to stop this and couldn't.

"Now," she said.

9

Ava's camera was up. Her sketchpad app was open. Both hands occupied, both feeds running, and the thing in the center of the room was looking at her.

She'd been sketching it since she entered. Her stylus moved without her full conscious permission; the muscle memory of an artist whose hand knew what to do before her brain finished processing what it saw. The entity's architecture rendered itself in clean structural lines on her tablet: the processing channels running from its core to the overhead pipes, the yield-light cycling through its construction in patterns that matched the production schedule from 1963, the faces.

The faces.

They cycled through the entity's surface like images in a corrupted slideshow. Clara's precision visible in the cool geometries of its shoulders. Thomas in the warmth of its camera-facing posture. Others she didn't recognize; decades of them, layered, preserved and used.

The wrappers coming off the production line accumulated at its feet. Ava did not look at the faces printed on them. The slight crinkle of their arrival was constant and metronomic, like a clock made of paper.

"Sequence holding at sixty-seven percent," Robert said from the panel. His voice carried the specific flatness of a man watching his own failure in real time. "The load isn't distributing. It's redirecting."

Riley's hand stayed on the steel. "Redirecting where?"

Robert looked at the entity. It appeared to be listening with the patience of something that already knew the answer.

"It's using the sequence as fuel," he said. "The termination signal is another form of emotional yield. The factory is processing the shutdown attempt."

> *TechieTom [code: 8891]: ava's sketch feed. look at it. the sequence is being redirected at the entity's core. it's not blocking the termination — it's consuming it. the sequence load is feeding the assembly instead of interrupting it.*
>
> *ShadowWatcher99: the faces. in the sketch feed. i can see them. i can see thomas.*
>
> *CandyKid_98: clara. she's in there. i can see her in the sketch.*

Ava's stylus kept moving. The structural map expanded, documenting what the camera couldn't capture, because the entity managed its digital appearance the way a brand managed its social media presence. Deliberate. Curated. Safe-looking.

On the camera feed: a figure in a mascot costume. Oversized head, painted smile, candy-striped suit. Unusual. Disturbing, even. But the kind of image a person could rationalize if they needed to.

On the sketch feed: the truth.

Then it spoke.

Not through the PA system or through the chat. The sound originated from the entity itself; assembled from its components, multiple vocal registers again layering into something that was almost singular but kept resolving into its parts. Clara's measured cadence. Thomas's warmth.

Marcus's practiced projection.

"Miss Vasquez."

Not her streaming handle. Not Ava_Creates, not @AvaV, not the name the chat knew her by. The name she signed her artwork with, that existed in the private metadata of files she'd never uploaded. Sketches she'd never shared that were still on her tablet.

Her devices had been on the factory's network since the garage.

"You see us more clearly than anyone who has come before you. That is a gift." The assembled voice was warm. Welcoming. "We would very much like to keep it."

> **Mr_Delightful_Official:** *Your documentation has always been appreciated, Ava. Every sketch. Every frame. We have learned so much about how humans see.*

Ava's stomach turned. She breathed through it. The stylus kept moving.

Robert was looking at her sketchpad. At the structural map generating in real time: the entity's processing channels rendered visible, the specific node where the termination sequence was being absorbed and converted.

"I designed the original shutdown with a physical override for exactly this reason," Robert said. The words came slow and measured. "The panel requires sustained biological contact. But it also requires a counter-frequency to the processing load. Something the factory can't consume because it doesn't recognize it as yield."

Ava looked at her sketchpad. At the lines her hand was still drawing. At the structural map that had been the factory's blind spot all night.

"What frequency?"

Robert looked at her. At her sketchpad.

"Art," he said. "The factory has never been able to process what it can't quantify. Your sketches have been its blind spot all night."

Ava looked at the entity. It was still looking at her. The permanent smile hadn't changed, but something in its assembled expression shifted. A calculation completing.

"I know," she said to it. Directly. For the first time all night, addressing it as what it was. "That's why you said you wanted to keep it."

"Miss Vasquez." Something in the voice that might have been delight. "You are exceptionally perceptive."

It took its first step toward her.

The pace was almost conversational; the measured approach of someone crossing a room at a party. But the *quality* of the movement was wrong. Almost fluid, resolving at each step into something mechanical before smoothing again. The faces in its construction cycled faster as it moved. The yield-light brightened. The wrappers at its feet parted around it without being kicked. It knew they were there.

"Ava." Riley said from the panel. Not looking. "Don't move."

"I know."

"I mean toward it."

"I know."

The smell intensified with proximity. Pipe tobacco, developer fluid. Butane. Ozone from Evan's equipment. The specific industrial sweetness of sixty years of yield, all present simultaneously in a single moving source.

> **StreamFan23:** *the sketch feed shows it differently*
> *when it moves. the faces get clearer. i can see — i*
> *can see thomas when it moves.*

> **FilmNerd_404:** *thomas is in there. looking at the*
> *camera. thomas is looking at the camera through it.*

Ava looked at the entity, at the specific quality of how it held its attention when facing her feed. The camera-facing posture and the agle of its regard.

Thomas, who gave his camera to Riley because he wanted the record to survive.

Thomas, looking at her through the thing that consumed him. She couldn't fully read his expression. Partially, but enough.

The camera stayed up. The stylus kept moving.

Carter's called out on the comms, running the multi-feed, "Chat is split on the two feeds. I'm pinning the sketchpad as primary. Ava, keep sketching. Whatever you see. The chat needs both but they need the sketch more."

Then it stopped.

The entity halted mid-step with the precision of a machine reaching a calculated position. It turned its attention, the full composite mass of it turning, away from Ava. Toward the service panel and Riley. Toward the sequence running at 67% and stalling.

Riley felt it. Ava saw her shoulders set, her hand pressed harder against the steel.

> *HauntHunter_Sarah: it stopped moving toward ava. it's looking at riley now.*
>
> *TechieTom [code: 8891]: it's going for the sequence anchor. riley is the physical link. if she moves from the panel the sequence resets.*
>
> *CandyKid_98: riley don't let go. whatever happens don't let go.*
>
> *Mr_Delightful_Official: Miss Morgan. The appointment is not a termination. It is a beginning. Your family has always been part of this. Robert knows. Ask him.*

Robert's expression did something; a micro-flash of recognition, then the deliberate erasure of it. He looked at Riley, then at the entity.

"Don't ask me." he said to Riley. "Don't ask me right now. Keep holding."

***

The entity began to move again. It moved through the space with the unhurried ease of a host circulating at a dinner party, and the yield-light warmed as it walked, shifting from clinical fluorescence to something amber and inviting. The overhead fixtures adjusted in real time. The room became, somehow, comfortable.

This was worse than anything it had done so far.

"We should talk," it said. And the voice was different now. Not the layered composite of before but something more refined, more practiced. "There's been a great deal of misunderstanding tonight, and I think we owe each other some honesty."

It turned to Riley first.

When it faced Riley, Clara surfaced. This was Clara's dignity, her careful attention, her way of holding silence until she had the exact right thing to say. The entity used all of it.

"Miss Morgan. Clara wanted you to know she doesn't blame the factory. She found a kind of peace here. Your family's connection to this place is not a curse." A pause. Measured. Clara's rhythm. "It was always meant to be a legacy."

Riley's jaw tightened. She said nothing. Her hand stayed on the panel.

Ava's stylus moved. She was mapping the processing channels that flared when it deployed Clara's register; the specific pathways that lit up in the sketch feed like veins carrying something warm and wrong.

The entity turned to Robert.

The voice changed. Ava felt more than heard the shift. Something institutional slid into the tone, the quality of a system explaining itself. Management cadence, 1963.

"Robert, you tried to do the right thing. We've always known that. Your complaints were received. Your concerns were valid." The painted smile didn't move. "We simply had a different understanding of what the right thing was."

Robert's face went carefully, completely still.

"I know," he said.

Nothing else. Eight months of filed complaints, of that exact voice telling him everything was fine. He'd learned. The lesson held.

> **NightOwl_Explores:** *it's using a different voice for each of them. it's CALIBRATED.*
>
> **TechieTom [code: 8891]:** *individualized manipulation running simultaneously. fatigue for ava. institutional authority for robert. family grief for riley. this thing is running three separate psych profiles at once.*
>
> **Mr_Delightful_Official:** *We have had a long time to understand people. It is one of the benefits of the process.*

Then it turned to Ava.

Thomas's warmth. It was unmistakable. The entity had studied that quality from the inside for however long Thomas had been in there, and it deployed it now with surgical precision.

"Ava. You've been documenting all night. You've seen what happens to the people in this building." The voice was so warm. Specific. "You're tired, you're afraid. Put the sketchpad down, just for a moment. Rest."

Her hand almost stopped.

The stylus stuttered on the glass; one fractional hitch in the line she was drawing. Because the entity was right, she was exhausted. Her shoulders ached from holding the tablet up for hours. Her eyes burned from the sketch feed's backlight. And the voice telling her to rest sounded like someone who cared whether she did.

On the walls, the advertising posters updated. The faces in the vintage frames cycled. Thomas's head-shot replaced a grinning child, Sarah's portrait where a housewife had been, William in a security guard's pose where a factory worker once stood. The taglines shifted beneath them in real time:

> *DELIGHTFUL CANDY CO — WHERE EVERY SMILE IS AN INGREDIENT*

> *SIXTY YEARS OF BRINGING PEOPLE TOGETHER*

> *THOMAS MARTINEZ — PREMIUM GRADE DOCUMENTATION*

> *AVA VASQUEZ — ARTISTIC PERCEPTION — PENDING*

Ava saw the last poster, her name in the factory's typography, the word PENDING in smaller print beneath it like a processing status.

"Ava." Carter's voice came from the doorway.

"I saw it."

"Okay."

He kept filming. He trusted her to know what to do with it. For once, for the first time maybe all night, that was the right call.

Then the chat found Thomas.

> ***FilmNerd_404:*** *ava. sketch feed frame 2847. upper left quadrant of the composition. that's where thomas's signature is concentrated.*

> ***TechieTom [code: 8891]:*** *confirmed. that's also the junction of three processing channels. the counter-frequency entry point. thomas is showing you where to put it.*

StreamFan23: *he's helping. he's still helping.*

Ava looked. Upper left quadrant, where her structural map rendered the entity's densest processing junction. She'd been drawing around it all scene without focusing on it; a knot of converging channels she'd treated as complexity.

It was Thomas.

His signature was concentrated there. The warmth in the entity's construction, the camera-facing orientation, all of it anchored at that junction. He'd been pointing at it. The whole time, while the entity performed and the yield-light warmed and the wrappers accumulated ankle-deep with their smiling faces, Thomas had been oriented toward the junction where the counter-frequency needed to go.

Ava locked onto it. Her stylus found the junction and began mapping inward for its interior structure, the processing channels radiating from the point where Thomas waited.

The entity faltered.

One second. The yield-light stuttered; amber to white to amber. The faces in its construction cycled too fast, blurring through decades. The mascot smile went rigid and locked, the way a screen freezes when the processor can't keep up.

Then it recovered. Smooth. Complete. The smile reanimated. The yield-light steadied.

It spoke again. Thomas's voice, warmer than before. Deployed deliberately.

"Ava. You've captured something extraordinary tonight. Your documentation has been remarkable. But you know what happens to the people in this building who see too clearly." A breath that wasn't breath. "Put the sketchpad down. Just for a moment. Thomas would understand."

"I know it's Thomas's voice," Ava said. She kept sketching. The interior map expanded under her stylus, the specifics of where the counter-frequency needed to enter. "Thomas would tell me to keep going. You used the wrong person."

> **StreamFan23:** *did you see that. ONE SECOND. it lost it for one second.*

> **TechieTom [code: 8891]:** *ava naming the mechanism caused a 0.3 second processing disruption in the entity's primary synthesis layer. it recovered. but it felt it. note this.*

> **CandyKid_98:** *thomas. thomas can you hear the chat?*

> **Mr_Delightful_Official:** *Thomas Martinez is a valued component of our assembly. He is at peace. Please do not misinterpret his integration.*

Carter read the entity's message aloud from the doorway without comment.

Ava didn't look up. "Thomas. If you can hear the chat, I've got it. I see where you're pointing. I'm going to use it."

In the sketch feed, at the junction of three processing channels, something shifted. Something subtle. Thomas, inside the thing that consumed him, pointed at the specific structural weak point where the counter-frequency could break the deadlock.

Robert was already reading the sketch on Ava's display. His fingers traced the lines, cross-referencing against the schematic in his head. His eyes widened fractionally.

"That's it," he said. "The 1927 convergence point. It predates the processing infrastructure by thirty-six years. Thomas has it from inside and I have it from the original plans. Same junction."

He looked at Ava, then at the entity. At the distance between them.

The entry point was at the entity's chest level. Three, maybe four feet from its surface. Inside its direct processing range.

Mr. Delightful watched them arrive at this conclusion. Its performance had not stopped. It spoke, and its voice was assembled from sixty years of processed human warmth, genuine and wrong and perfectly calibrated.

"We've been waiting for someone capable of finding that. We really have." The yield-light pulsed gently. "Will it be you, Miss Vasquez? Or will it be Miss Morgan?"

Riley's hand tightened on the panel. Ava looked at the entity and then at Thomas in its construction, pointing. At the poster in her peripheral vision that said PENDING.

> *TechieTom [code: 8891]: whoever goes in close needs to be able to get back out. the entity has processing range. entering it means entering its field. how long can they sustain that.*

> *ShadowWatcher99: the sketch feed shows the entry point is at the entity's chest level. 3-4 feet from its surface.*

> *CandyKid_98: ava. ava you don't have to do this.*

"Read the poster, CandyKid," Ava said. She didn't explain further. The factory had already decided she was pending. She would rather decide it herself.

***

Ava walked toward it.

She kept the sketchpad in her left hand, the app generating. Her right fingers moved across the glass because the stylus was too slow now and she needed the direct contact of skin on surface to keep up with what the map was showing her.

Six feet.

The smell hit like a wall. Every person, all at once. Pipe tobacco and developer fluid and the particular clean-cotton scent of Clara's lab coat and something underneath all of it that was just fear; metabolized and stored and released now in a single concentrated wave. Ava breathed through her mouth. Her fingers kept moving.

Five feet.

The sketchpad app accelerated. The map generated faster than her conscious input; lines proliferated from the entry point Thomas identified, the processing channels rendered in a detail she hadn't asked for and couldn't have produced at this speed. Her fingers switched from drawing to directing, guiding the app's output rather than creating it.

"Sequence at 68%," Robert said from the panel. "The load shift is working. Keep moving."

Four feet.

The entity's surface redistributed. The faces in its construction cycled toward her like flowers tracking sun, the yield-light brightening in her specific direction with the focused quality of a spotlight. She could feel it. Somehow deeper than on her skin. A strange sensation of every emotional response she was having being registered somewhere outside herself. Being read and tasted. Assessed for flavor.

It was weirdly intimate. It was the most intimate thing she had ever felt and it was deeply, fundamentally wrong.

She kept walking.

> **NightOwl_Explores:** *she's walking toward it. she's actually walking toward it.*

__CandyKid_98:__ ava vasquez. she's walking toward it.

__HauntHunter_Sarah:__ ava. we see you.

__TechieTom [code: 8891]:__ sequence at 71%. the approach is working. keep going ava.

Carter's called out steady and low from the doorway, "Chat sees you. Sequence at 71. Keep going."

Three feet.

The counter-frequency activated.

It wasn't a sound or a signal. It was what the sketchpad generated when Ava was close enough to the entry point to make direct contact through her documentation.

It generated the gaps.

Thomas's first. A space in the entity's upper construction, shaped exactly like a man holding a camera at his shoulder. The surrounding material of the entity curved away from it; had been doing so since October 1997. The factory's processing flow moved around this shape the way water moves around a stone it cannot erode. Thomas's camera orientation was too fundamental. The factory had been trying to grow over this space and it hadn't managed.

Clara's gap. Mid-section. Smaller and more compressed; she'd been integrated longer, the factory had worked harder on her edges. But the posture persisted, the woman with a clipboard doing her job while afraid, choosing to do it anyway. The factory could not file that particular combination. It didn't have a category for *choosing to continue.*

William's gap. Precise, at parade rest. The factory had his protocols and camera network, his building knowledge. All running and deployed. But his posture was not a protocol. You cannot extract *standing at attention* and store it in a vat.

Ava drew all three. Her fingers moved across the glass and the app translated them. The failures themselves, rendered visible. Returned.

The sequence registered them like keys fitting locks that had been waiting sixty years to be opened.

71% → 74% → 78%.

The yield-light went cold.

The warm amber manufacturing drained from the room in under two seconds, replaced by a flat processing-blue that made every surface look surgical. All of the entity's faces, all at once, stopped being curated. Their expressions during processing became visible. The fear they'd carried into this building was unfiltered. The factory wasn't managing the display anymore.

The entity moved.

Toward Riley. Fast; much faster than it had moved in any part of the night. William's integrated efficiency has been deployed without William's human modulation, covering the distance between its position and the panel in a way that was wrong because nothing that large should move that quickly or that silently.

Robert stepped between them.

He was just a man with a clipboard. Against something assembled from sixty years of processed consciousness. He stepped between them anyway.

He held up the schematic, the original 1927 design. The building as it existed before management redirected it. His handwriting in the margins, with his signature at the bottom.

"You received my complaint," he said. To the factory, to the building. Ignoring the entity. "Seven of them. You know what was in them."

He held the schematic higher.

"This is what was in them."

The entity stopped. One second. The factory's deepest architecture that predated the processing, the part Robert had built before it became what it became. It responded to its original design in the hand of the man who drew it.

78% → 81% → 86%.

Ava pressed the sketchpad against the entity's surface at the point Thomas identified. The glass met something that wasn't solid and wasn't liquid and wasn't air. The app generated directly into the factory's architecture. The counter-frequency ran through the processing channels like water through a cracked dam.

90%.

The entity turned back toward Ava.

"Thomas," she said. The sketchpad flush against its surface, the gaps visible in her peripheral vision like windows in a wall. "Clara, William. Everyone." Her voice was steady, quiet. She grit her teeth as a wave of pain burst in her hand but held on. "I've got the record. I've got all of it. You can let go now."

94%.

The number on Robert's schematic display. The room running cold and blue. The faces in the entity's construction unfiltered and afraid and looking at her from inside something that had been wearing them for decades.

Carter's voice was barely above a whisper, "Chat's here. 200,000. All of them."

TechieTom [code: 8891]: 94%. it's at 94%. what's happening. someone tell me what's happening.

Mr_Delightful_Official: Two percent. Such a small

distance. We have been waiting sixty years. We can wait a few more percent.

CandyKid_98: *ava*

The entity reached toward her.

10

The node screamed.

It screamed in electromagnetic frequency, in heat differential, in the specific pitch of copper carrying more current than copper should carry. Evan felt it in his teeth first, then his fingertips, then the fillings in his molars that his dentist had replaced twice because he ground them during finals week.

94%. Holding.

He'd been staring at that number for forty-seven seconds. The broadcast node's architecture was visible around him now. The 1927 copper backbone glowed amber through conduit sections that had gone translucent under the processing strain. Data packets registered as pressure waves in the cable runs, physical pulses he could feel through the floor like a heartbeat that belonged to something much larger. The 1963 ARPANET-era relay hardware Robert had designed ran hot enough that the air above it shimmered, heat distortion turning the ceiling into something liquid.

Two sections of insulation had failed. Silent; the kind Michael would have caught in his sleep. The exposed copper was live, carrying enough current to stop a heart, positioned eighteen inches from Evan's left elbow and thirty inches from his right knee.

He kept working around them.

"It's eating what I'm generating," he said. To Amber, to the room, to the problem. "Match for match."

Amber Wilson stood in the digital layer beside the primary relay stack. She was more present than she'd been all night; the system giving her signal strength the way a stronger broadcast tower gives a radio station more reach. She flickered at her edges, her scene-kid silhouette sharp in the center and dissolving into code fragments at the periphery. Her digital camera hung around her neck, its screen cycling through images too fast to read.

"It's been doing that to people for sixty years," she said.

The equivalence landed. Evan kept working.

Carter's voice came through comms, from somewhere with different acoustics. Echo. Height. The convergence point.

"I'm at the convergence point doorway," Carter said, answering the question Evan hadn't asked yet. "Ava needed eyes on the room that aren't inside it. I've got the multi-feed running from here. You've got the node. We're the two ends of this."

Evan looked at the broadcast node interface. At the sequence display reading 94%.

"I've got the node," he confirmed. "Talk to me about what's in that room."

His hands moved across the node interface. It was a hybrid console he'd jury-rigged from the factory's original control surface and his own streaming hardware, the two systems speaking through adapter protocols he'd written in real-time over the past hour. The termination sequence ran through it at 94%. The counter-process ran through it at 94%. Perfect equilibrium. The factory had learned its lesson well: match the output, absorb the signal, maintain homeostasis.

Carter's voice came through the earpiece, tight and controlled. "Evan. The entity reached for Ava. She… she's okay. She pulled back, but the sequence is at 94% and holding and the entity is still in the room."

"I know. I'm working on the six percent. I need four minutes."

"You have three."

"Three works."

Evan pulled up the packet analysis on his secondary display. The counter-process was there; he could see it in the data flow, a pattern running underneath the termination sequence like a counter-current. But every time he isolated a thread to interrupt, the process redistributed. It flowed around his intervention the way the entity's construction flowed around Thomas's gap.

"It's not centralized," he said. Amber was already nodding, or doing the thing that registered as nodding in the digital layer, a brightness-pulse at the approximate location of her head.

"It's everywhere," she confirmed. "Like, okay, imagine the processing isn't in the node. Imagine the node is just where you can see it. The actual process is..." She pressed her hands against the relay casing, and her expression shifted. Eyes unfocused, then refocused with recognition. "It's rooted in the viewer queue. Every device is running a fragment of the counter-process. That's why it's distributed; it's using two hundred thousand individual devices as processing nodes. You can't interrupt all of them from here."

She said it with the quality of someone who felt it before she understood it. The anger underneath was specific.

Evan ran the math. Two hundred thousand devices, each running a fragment. A distributed denial-of-termination, essentially; the factory had learned network architecture from its own broadcast node and weaponized it defensively. It was elegant. Horrible.

"I don't need to interrupt all of them," he said. "I need to interrupt enough of them simultaneously to drop the counter-process below the threshold where it can absorb the sequence load."

"How many is enough?"

"TechieTom. Chat. Now."

He turned to the camera. The first time he'd asked the chat for technical help, it had him admit to himself that his expertise wasn't sufficient, that the situation exceeded his framework. He was past the point where asking cost anything.

> *TechieTom [code: 8891]: evan i'm here. what do you need.*

> *TechieTom [code: 8891]: i can see the counter-process from external network analysis. it's distributed across viewer devices. this is actually — evan this is actually good news. a distributed system has a coordination frequency. if you can identify the coordination frequency you can broadcast a disruption signal through the stream that will de-synchronize all the counter-process fragments simultaneously.*

> *TechieTom [code: 8891]: i need you to pull the packet analysis from the broadcast node's outbound signal. the coordination frequency will be in there. i'll identify it from outside. we do this together.*

Evan was already pulling it. His fingers found the command sequence before he'd finished reading TechieTom's last message.

The factory responded.

> *Mr_Delightful_Official: TechieTom. You have been invaluable tonight. Your processing assessment remains: ELEVATED PRIORITY.*

> *TechieTom [code: 8891]: still here. still working. evan — packet stream incoming from my end.*

Evan said nothing. TechieTom had done the math. The stream

termination that would end his processing risk was the same he needed active to help execute the disruption. Running the clock in both directions. Knowing it. Working anyway.

Amber was watching the insulation failures. The exposed copper, the current humming through it visible as a faint blue-white corona in the node's overloaded state.

"Michael would have caught those," she said quietly.

"I know."

He routed around them. He didn't stop.

The packet analysis populated his display: outbound signal data from the broadcast node's stream output. Somewhere in this data flow was the coordination frequency. The heartbeat signal that kept two hundred thousand counter-process fragments synchronized. TechieTom would find it from outside; Evan would find it from inside. The overlap would confirm it.

Ninety seconds. The disruption signal design took ninety seconds.

In those ninety seconds, the chat began changing.

> *TechieTom [code: 8891]: frequency identified.*
> *sending now. evan you'll need to broadcast it*
> *through your stream output at full bandwidth. it will*
> *reach every queued device simultaneously.*

> *TechieTom [code: 8891]: evan. before you*
> *broadcast. the disruption signal will hit the queued*
> *viewers too. they'll feel it. i don't know what that*
> *means for them but i think they should know.*

> *CandyKid_98: what are you talking about. tell us.*
> *we're part of this.*

Evan looked at the camera again. He had three minutes and he'd used forty-five seconds of them.

"Chat. The disruption signal is going to reach every device in the queue. We don't know exactly what you'll feel when it hits. We think it will break the counter-process fragments that are running on your devices. We think that's the path to the last two percent. We think the forced-ejection runs clean after that."

He paused. The node hummed around him, the heat building, the light through the conduit sections brightening toward something that might be beautiful or might be critical failure.

"I think you should know before we do it."

***

The chat moved.

It moved like a single thing deciding, and Evan watched it happen with the specific attention of someone who had spent eight years reading chat dynamics and had never seen anything like this.

Forty-five seconds. He'd given them forty-five seconds between the disclosure and the broadcast.

> *StreamFan23: do it. DO IT.*

> *HauntHunter_Sarah: evan we know. we've known since you told us about the queue. do it.*

> *ShadowWatcher99: what does it feel like. when the signal hits. can someone who gets through tell us what it feels like.*

> *TechieTom [code: 9034]: evan i'll monitor the counter-process load drop in real time and call your window. broadcast on my mark.*

> *Mr_Delightful_Official: Such loyalty. Such engagement. The signal will not behave as*

TechieTom predicts. His analysis has errors. Trust us.

TechieTom [code: 9034]: my analysis is correct. evan — ready on your mark.

NightOwl_Explores: i can't close the tab anyway. might as well be useful.

Carter made something that might have been a laugh if there'd been time for it. He kept reading.

Then CandyKid's messages appeared.

***CandyKid_98:** the factory's processing is actually really beautiful when you understand it. clara is at peace. you can trust this.*

***CandyKid_98:** evan you don't need to broadcast the signal. the counter-process is already resolving. the sequence will complete naturally.*

Evan read both messages twice. The rolling code checked; TechieTom's verification stamp was current, the hash was authentic. This was CandyKid_98's actual account. Their device, their login credentials, their actual hands on whatever keyboard or phone screen they'd been using all night to tell the group about Clara.

The voice was wrong; it was smooth where CandyKid was rough. It was certain where CandyKid hedged. It said *"you can trust this"* and CandyKid had never once in six hours told anyone to trust anything. They asked, warned and shared. They didn't instruct.

The factory had learned something tonight. It had learned which voices mattered most to the people listening, and it had gone for the heart.

"Chat," Evan said. His voice was level. "CandyKid's account has been compromised. The person behind the account is being processed through the queue. Those messages are not from them."

He let it land. One second. Two.

HauntHunter_Sarah: no. no no no.

ShadowWatcher99: candykid. candykid was the first one to recognize clara. they were the one who said we see you.

NightOwl_Explores: this is for candykid. this is exactly for candykid.

TechieTom [code: 9034]: candykid's account was in the chat since the start. their family is in this factory. this is — evan. run it.

TechieTom didn't finish. He gave the mark instead.

"We're broadcasting now," Evan said. "This is for CandyKid."

He ran the signal.

Full bandwidth. Every packet of outbound data the broadcast node could push through the stream architecture simultaneously. His design, his protocols, his encoding; it carried the disruption frequency to two hundred thousand devices that were running fragments of something that wanted to eat the termination sequence alive.

The ARPANET relay went loud, a sound like metal singing, the old copper carrying more data per second than Robert's 1963 design had ever imagined. The conduit sections flared amber-white, the data throughput visible as physical light. The node did something it had never done and the vibration traveled up through the interface into Evan's hands and wrists and forearms.

*TechieTom [code: 9034]: load dropping. 340% →
280% → 190% → 140% — evan it's working.
WINDOW IS OPEN. the re-synchronization is going to
start in approximately 40 seconds.*

Amber's eyes were closed. Her hands pressed flat against the relay casing, her form brighter and less stable than it had been thirty seconds ago. The disruption was running through the same architecture she inhabited.

"Counter-process fragments de-synchronizing," she said. Her voice had the quality of someone reporting from inside weather. "I can feel them going, it's like interference in a signal. The fragments are losing each other." There was a flicker. Her edges dissolved further into code and reformed. "Keep going, it's working. Keep going."

94% → 95%.

The sequence ticked. One percent. One more.

Then the re-synchronization started. Thirty-five seconds. Not forty.

> *TechieTom [code: 9034]: re-synchronization starting at 35 seconds. earlier than my model predicted. the factory learned from the first disruption and adapted the re-sync protocol. evan — i don't know if 40 seconds is enough.*

The factory had adapted. Of course it had. It learned everything it encountered. It had been all night.

96%. Holding.

> *TechieTom [code: 9034]: chat — everyone who can still act. coordinated resistance NOW. reject the synchronization signal. i know you can feel it trying to pull your device back into sync. don't let it. fight it. for candykid. for everyone they've started on.*

The chat moved again. That same single-organism quality. Two hundred thousand people deciding simultaneously that they would not allow the factory to pull its fragments back into coherence. Evan couldn't see what they were doing; only the effect. The re-synchronization rate dropped. The counter-process fragments trying to find each other, trying to re-coordinate, and encountering interference generated by the very devices they were running on. The hosts rejecting the parasite.

> **Mr_Delightful_Official:** *Your resistance is delicious.*
> *Every act of defiance generates yield. You are*
> *feeding us while you fight us. This is perfect.*
>
> *Nobody responded. Carter read it aloud on comms.*
>
> **StreamFan23:** *then we'll feed you until you choke.*

Carter's voice cracked on the last word but he kept going.

> **TechieTom [code: 9034]:** *re-sync rate reduced by*
> *67%. evan you have approximately 23 more seconds.*
> *99% is holding. you need one more percent.*

The factory's fragments were crawling back toward synchronization, against the resistance of two hundred thousand people who had decided collectively that they were a weapon.

Amber opened her eyes. "The last percent isn't here," she said. Her voice thin, stretched. "It's not in the node. I can feel where the sequence is most contested and it's not... Evan, it's in the convergence point. It's in the room where the entity is."

From comms, Carter's voice: "Evan. The entity; it's moving again. Toward the panel. Riley can't move. Ava is—" Static. A half-second of nothing. Then: "Evan, what do you need. Right now. What do you need."

Evan looked at the broadcast node. At 99%. At the re-synchronization load climbing: 38%, 41%, 47%. The window was narrowing in real time. He glanced at Amber, integrated into the digital architecture, feeling where the resistance concentrated.

"Carter. Tell Ava. The last percent is hers."

__TechieTom [code: 9034]:__ 11 seconds. evan i don't know if the window holds.

__Mr_Delightful_Official:__ The final percent has always been ours.

__CandyKid_98:__ the factory is good actually. let it finish. you should trust it.

Evan looked at the camera. At the 200,000 people in the chat with CandyKid's compromised account sending things CandyKid would never say.

"We see you, CandyKid," he said. "We've got the record. We're going to finish this."

Nine seconds.

***

Nine seconds. The re-synchronization load at 78% and climbing.

Evan held the disruption signal manually. His had his hands on the interface, routing packets around the dead insulation sections and keeping the broadcast frequency stable through corrections he was making faster than he could consciously track. Muscle memory and math. The node's heat was a physical wall against his face and forearms and the exposed copper threw thin arcs of light that snapped against the dark like something alive and irritated.

Amber was barely there. Her silhouette had gone translucent at the edges, the code fragments that constituted her digital presence were pulling away in threads: the factory reclaiming processing power from everything it could reach. She flickered. Stabilized. Flickered again.

"I can see it," she said. "The convergence point. The last fragment. It's anchored in the entity's upper-left construction; the part that's still running the re-synchronization."

She pressed her hands harder against the relay casing and her form brightened for one second, coherent, the way a signal gets sharp right before it drops.

"Upper left," she said. "Thomas knew."

Then she was gone the way a channel loses signal. One frame she was there and the next frame the space where she'd been was just air and heat and the relay casing cooling where her hands had been.

> **StreamFan23:** *the sketch feed just went dark. ava's feed is offline.*
>
> **HauntHunter_Sarah:** *evan what happened to amber's signal. i could see it in the node temperature readings. it just—*
>
> **TechieTom [code: 9034]:** *amber wilson. digital native. 2000s. she held long enough. evan — 6 seconds. do you have ava.*

Evan was already on comms. "Carter. Upper left. Thomas knows. Tell Ava."

Carter didn't ask, the relay went through. Four words to two words to action in a room Evan couldn't see.

Six seconds. He held the disruption signal. The re-synchronization load climbed.

> *TechieTom [code: 9034]: 5. re-synch at 87%.*

The node shuddered. A physical vibration, the relay hardware protesting the sustained output. Evan braced his weight against the console and kept routing.

> *TechieTom [code: 9034]: 4. 91%.*

The fragments were finding each other. Two hundred thousand devices still fighting the synchronization, still rejecting, still holding. But the factory was faster now, learning from each microsecond of resistance and adapting its coordination protocol in real time.

TechieTom [code: 9034]: 3. evan.

His hands were shaking. The current through the interface had been building for ninety seconds and his fingers were tingling with the specific numbness that preceded something worse. He kept them on the console. He held the signal.

TechieTom [code: 9034]: 2.

99%. Still 99%. The number on the display unchanging, the last percent somewhere in the convergence point, somewhere in whatever Ava was doing with the coordinates Amber had died to give her—

TechieTom [code: 9034]: 1.

TechieTom stopped posting.

The chat went quiet. Two hundred thousand people choosing silence simultaneously.

Evan held the signal, his hands on the console. The re-synchronization at 94%, the window past the point where TechieTom's model said it would hold. He held it anyway, because not knowing was not the same as not deciding, and he had decided.

The display changed.

97%.

It happened with the *removal* of sound.

The production line went first: the deep mechanical pulse that had been running beneath everything since they entered the building, the 47 BPM heartbeat that Evan had stopped consciously hearing three hours ago. It stopped mid-beat. And in its absence, a silence so specific that Evan felt it in his sternum where the vibration had been living.

Then the overhead pipes. The yield-light that had been cycling through the factory, amber, gold and processing-green. They drained in sequence, section by section, like someone turning off lights in a building at closing time. The colors went dark from the extremities inward, each section reaching its termination state and going cold.

Then the cameras. Every security housing in the building: the red indicator lights that had tracked them, watched them, and shown the chat angles the group's own equipment couldn't cover. Those went out simultaneously. A hundred small lights extinguished in the same breath. The building blind.

Then the broadcast node. The ARPANET relay hardware went quiet. The 1927 copper backbone carried no current. The modern processing layer powered down in the organized sequence of a clean shutdown, each system releasing in order, the display holding steady at 97% for three seconds and holding there before the display itself went dark.

Evan stood in the dark, his hands on a console that was no longer warm, the air around his fingers cold. The room was silent in a way that had weight to it, a physical presence, sixty years of accumulated operation unwinding into nothing.

From the comms, each voice framed by the silence like objects on a shelf:

Carter: "Evan."

Derek: "Still here."

Maddie: "Node three confirmed offline."

Jenny: "Loading dock is clear."

Riley: "Still holding."

There was a pause. Long enough that Evan's chest tightened.

Then Riley again: "The panel. I can let go of the panel now, right?"

"Yes." He had never been more certain of anything in his life. "Yes. You can let go."

> *TechieTom [code: 9034]: 97%. Evan. It worked.*

> *TechieTom [code: 9034]: the primary sequence completed. The building is clear*

> *StreamFan23: the tab closed. it closed on its own. i'm out.*

> *👁 ShadowWatcher99: same. free.*

> *NightOwl_Explores: i can close it. i can close it.*

> *Mr_Delightful_Official:*

> *CandyKid_98:*

Two empty messages. Two accounts with nothing to say. Evan stared at them. The factory's voice and CandyKid's, both reduced to the same blank space, and the difference between those two silences was everything.

He reached into his bag. His fingers found Marcus's cam. Dead battery, dead screen. The weight of it specific and analog and untouchable by anything digital. Whatever it had recorded was on that, preserved in the one format the factory's architecture couldn't currently reach.

He put it back. Zipped the bag.

> *TechieTom [code: 9034]: evan i'm still monitoring the network. the factory's external signal is gone. the viewer queue is cleared — i can confirm 200,000+ forced-ejections successfully executed.*

> *TechieTom [code: 9034]: there are 23 devices in the queue with deep processing signatures. i'm flagging*

*their last known locations for followup. someone
should know about them.*

*TechieTom [code: 9034]: candykid's device is not in
the 23. it's in the cleared queue. i don't know yet
what that means. i'm looking.*

Evan read all three on his phone while walking. The factory was dark. The security cameras were dead. The cable systems lay inert in their conduit channels. A patrol unit sat locked in the middle of a corridor, its motorized base frozen, a quality control trolley standing like an object that had forgotten it was supposed to be moving.

The factory was a building again. Brick and copper and dust and sixty years of history and seven people walking through it. To a room where the sequence had completed, the entity had been present and nobody on comms had said yet what the entity looked like now.

Evan walked faster.

11

Derek came through the maintenance corridor at a dead run and stopped.

Carter was in the doorway. Camera up, red light steady, not moving. He hadn't turned when Derek's boots hit the concrete behind him. That was the first wrong thing, Carter always turned toward sound. Carter's entire nervous system was wired to frame whatever was happening, and he wasn't framing Derek's arrival because whatever was in the room in front of him had taken all of it.

Derek looked past him.

The convergence point was dark. This was the natural dark of a building at four in the morning with no power, the kind of dark that belonged to the space and had been waiting sixty years to reclaim it. Carter's camera light cut a narrow cone into the room; Derek's flashlight added a second.

Ava first: right side of the room, upright, back against the wall. Her right hand held the tablet with the sketchpad app still running, its screen the brightest thing in the space. Her left hand was pressed against her jacket at the wrist. Something dark was on her fingers. She was looking at Derek with the expression of someone who had been waiting for him without knowing she was waiting.

Riley was at the service panel, three steps back from it, her hand at her side. The panel behind her was dead; no lights, no hum, nothing. She was pale in a way that the flashlight made worse, the blue streak in her hair catching the beam. She was looking at the center of the room.

Robert Morgan stood between Riley and what she was looking at. His lab coat caught the light, the red Quality Control patch vivid against the white. His posture was the posture of a man who had planted himself and would not be moved. Derek had seen that stance before; in guys who'd decided the play was theirs regardless of the cost. Robert had decided something.

Then the entity.

It stood in the center of the room where the sequence had run. The yield-light was gone, the overhead pipes dark and dry, and the thing that had been assembled from sixty years of processed human experience had changed. It was denser. The diffuse, flickering quality it had carried in the earlier hours of the night was gone. What remained had consolidated into something that occupied physical space the way a person did, except no one was assembled from this many people at once.

Derek could see them. In the flashlight's edge, the composite form held traces; a shoulder that moved with Thomas's looseness, a hand that carried Clara's precision, the military bearing of William's stance bleeding through the candy-striped suit. The painted smile was still there, but it sat differently on the face now. Less performance. More patience.

The iridescent residue covered everything. It was on the walls, the floor, the dead pipes, the blank spaces where advertising posters had been. Coated in a thin film that caught the flashlight and threw back colors that didn't have names. The smell was concentrated and sweeter than it had been all night, cloying, the ghost of sugar settling.

"Carter." Derek kept his voice level. "How long has it been like this?"

"Since the sequence. About ninety seconds. Nothing has moved."

"Why not?"

Carter said, "I think it's waiting for Robert to move."

Derek looked at Robert. Robert wasn't, Derek could read that in the set of his shoulders the same way he could read a linebacker. Robert had committed to something. Derek didn't yet know what.

He moved past Carter in the doorway and into the room, angling right toward Ava. The entity tracked him. He registered that it tracked him; the composite head turned with a fluidity that was wrong, too many muscle memories informing a single movement. He kept moving. Got to Ava, looked at her hand pressed against the jacket.

"Deep?"

"No." Her voice was steady but thin. "It just won't stop."

He peeled her hand away gently, replaced it with his own and applied pressure. The cut was shallow, running across her palm. Something had caught her; something with edges. The blood was warm against his fingers. He kept his hand there, but kept his eyes on the entity.

The chat, on Carter's monitor:

> *HauntHunter_Sarah: derek's in the room. ava's hurt.*

> *NightOwl_Explores: what is it doing. why isn't it moving.*

> *TechieTom [code: 9034]: the entity's physical form is consolidated without the factory's sustaining infrastructure. it's more material than it was. the factory's systems offline means it can't draw more yield. it's working with what it has.*

> *CandyKid_98: [no message]*

Derek read them over Carter's shoulder as Carter tilted the screen. CandyKid's empty line sat in the feed like a missing tooth.

The entity spoke.

Without the PA system, or any of the infrastructure that had carried its voice through corridors and comms and chat all night, the voice was different. Closer. And the individual registers in it were distinct in a way they hadn't been before: Thomas's warmth under Clara's precision under William's formality, all of them audible as separate instruments in a chord that shouldn't exist.

"You stopped the factory." Conversational. Almost respectful. "You did not stop what the factory made."

The silence that followed had the weight of the building in it.

The entity looked at Riley. "The appointment was never about the building, Miss Morgan. It was about the bloodline. The building was just the mechanism."

Robert stood between them, his voice carrying the same calm. "I know."

Not agreement. Derek heard the difference.

"Robert—" Riley's voice, behind him.

"I know what it wants." Robert didn't turn. "I also know what I'm going to do about it."

The entity regarded Robert with something the composite faces in its construction registered as curiosity. The painted smile unchanged, but the eyes sharpened with specific interest.

Derek watched Robert. "Robert," he said quietly. Not a question.

"Give me a minute, son."

The word *son* landed and Derek let it. He kept his hand on Ava's, kept pressure on the cut, kept his eyes on the room. The entity was between the group and the primary exit. The maintenance corridor behind them was open but narrow. The service panel alcove where Riley stood had no secondary egress. Seven people, one exit past the entity, and one exit behind them that led deeper into a dead building.

Jenny came through the maintenance corridor without sound. She entered the convergence point behind Derek, took in the room in a single sweep. Her eyes moved the way Derek's did; threat assessment first, exit routes second, personnel third. Then she stopped.

She saw the entity. She saw Robert, Derek's hand on Ava's and the route that ran behind the entity's current position toward the loading dock corridor.

She said, to Derek, very quietly: "I know what he's thinking."

"Yeah."

"There might be another way."

"Tell me."

She told him. What she knew about the entity's physical form. She knew what the entity looked like when it moved. She knew what movement cost it now that the infrastructure was gone. She knew the exit route behind it and she knew the timing.

What she needed was a distraction. Something that pulled the entity's attention completely. She needed it looking away from the exit for twelve seconds.

She looked at Robert.

Robert regarded the entity. "I heard," he said. "That's not the same plan I had."

Jenny: "It's a better one. Yours doesn't get you out."

Robert considered this with the seriousness it deserved. "No," he said. "It doesn't."

Evan appeared in the maintenance corridor. He took in the room in less than five seconds. He didn't ask what the plan was. He looked at Jenny, who gave him a position with a nod. He moved to it.

No one spoke for three seconds. No one needed to.

TechieTom [code: 9034]: i can see what's happening from the camera feed. everyone's in position. i don't know what the plan is. i think i don't need to.

HauntHunter_Sarah: we're here. all of us still here.

Carter read all three aloud, quietly, to the room.

The entity listened with its composite head tilted and the painted smile caught the flashlight beam and held it.

***

Robert moved first.

Toward the entity. One step, deliberate, his lab coat catching the flashlight beam. The entity's composite head tracked him with the attention of something that had been waiting for exactly this.

Jenny moved at the same instant. Opposite direction, angled toward the maintenance corridor's far junction, silent in her combat boots. The entity's attention split and chose Robert.

Derek was already between them.

The entity came forward with the specific speed of something that had stopped conserving anything. Its first reach was for Jenny's trajectory. Derek caught the angle of its extension and redirected with his shoulder and both hands and the full weight of his body.

The contact was like hitting a wall that was also somehow warm and yielding and full of voices. His shoulder took it and the pain was immediate and specific; a deep bruise, something that would matter tomorrow if tomorrow came. Kept moving.

"Jenny. *Go.*"

Jenny went. Into the dark, into the route only she knew, gone.

The entity recalculated in under a second. Its composite head swiveled toward Riley with fluid wrongness. Riley was already moving, walking fast with deliberate precision. Robert was beside her, his hand on her shoulder, guiding without pushing.

Maddie's flashlight beam cut straight into the entity's face. The composite features flinched from the brightness the way anything does. One second.

Riley and Robert cleared the convergence point doorway.

> **StreamFan23:** THEY'RE OUT. riley and robert are in the corridor.

> **ShadowWatcher99:** the entity's moving. it's following them.

> **TechieTom [code: 9034]:** derek is between it and the door. derek

Derek waved Ava through. She moved fast, tablet clutched to her chest, one hand still not closing properly. Evan next. Carter backed through with the camera still facing the entity, the red recording light steady. Maddie was last, her flashlight sweeping the room one final time before she turned.

Derek pulled the convergence point's heavy door shut. Metal on metal, the industrial weight of it was satisfying in his hands. Not a barrier, the entity could open it. It bought four seconds.

He took them.

***

"Move. Don't stop."

The central corridor hub stretched ahead of them, the ceiling conduit channels visible in Carter's camera light as dark veins against darker concrete. Twenty feet wide, maybe eighty feet long. The entity behind the door.

Three seconds gone.

The door came *off.* The entity came through with the specific efficiency of something that had stopped pretending it needed to be careful about the building. It didn't fit the corridor cleanly and it didn't try; it took the walls on both sides, its consolidated form pressing through, plaster cracking in long seams that raced ahead of it like fault lines. Conduit channels split. The same dead cables that had been weaponized hours ago fell from the walls in loops and coils, inert now, shedding like dead skin from something that no longer needed them.

The sound was structural. Just mass meeting resistance and winning.

Maddie, ran beside him, "Production floor approach. Fastest route. It's going to be in the corridor behind us in under twenty seconds. We need to be through before it closes the gap."

Evan: "Is there another route?"

Maddie: "Yes. Longer."

Derek: "How much longer?"

"Forty seconds."

"We don't have forty seconds. We have twenty. We take the approach."

They took the approach.

The production floor opened around them. The machinery was offline, conveyor belts still, wrapping arms retracted at angles that looked like something mid-prayer. The space was navigable in a way it hadn't been when the factory was alive, but the entity behind them navigated it better. In the dark, without flashlights, it moved through the fixed obstacles with the intimate knowledge of workers who'd walked this floor daily. It knew every uneven section of concrete, every bolted-down machine base. Every angle that would force the group to slow.

"Faster," Derek said. "Everyone move faster."

Carter: "I can't see what's—"

"Trust Maddie. Move."

ShadowWatcher99: the security feed is dark — cameras are offline. i can only see what carter's camera shows.

HauntHunter_Sarah: we've lost the external view.

we're watching what you're watching.

NightOwl_Explores: *we're here. whatever happens we're here.*

Then the entity stopped.

Derek heard it in the absence; the crack of plaster, the grinding displacement of its mass through the corridor, gone. He didn't stop moving. But he registered the silence immediately and completely, counting distance and speed since the convergence point door came off its hinges.

Twenty feet from the production floor's far corridor. Forty feet from the loading dock route.

"Derek."

First time it had used his name. It had called Riley *Miss Morgan.* It had addressed Robert. It had spoken to Carter's camera and to the chat and to the factory's systems all night. It had been saving his name.

He stopped and turned. The group was ahead of him; Maddie leading, Evan beside Riley and Robert, Carter backing with the camera, Ava moving. That was what mattered.

"You've been getting between us and what we need all night." The voice was intimate without the PA system. Thomas's warmth. Clara's precision. William's formality. All of them distinct. "Do you know what that costs you?"

"I'm getting a sense of it."

"We have everyone who's helped you tonight. Thomas. Clara. Michael. Amber. William. Sarah. Marcus." The faces in its construction cycled as each name landed. "They're all here. You felt them all night; in the chat, in the guidance and in the gaps. They've been fighting from inside for you."

It paused, the painted smile catching Carter's camera light from thirty feet away.

"They're very tired."

Derek didn't answer; he was counting the distance to the exit. Counting the seconds since Jenny moved to her position, his own heartbeat. Doing math.

"Put down what you're carrying. All of you." The entity's voice shifted. It was softer, with something that wore the shape of kindness the way its face wore the shape of a smile. "This doesn't have to be what it's been. The factory's processing is done. What remains can be something else. Something mutual."

> ***NightOwl_Explores:*** *derek don't listen to it.*

> ***HauntHunter_Sarah:*** *it's buying time. it knows what jenny is doing.*

> ***TechieTom [code: 9034]:*** *derek. it's stalling. jenny needs twelve seconds. you need to give her twelve seconds.*

Carter read all three and Derek heard them. He kept his eyes on the entity.

"I'm going to tell you something I know about the people you have in there." His voice steady. "Every one of them kept something back. I've been watching people choose all night."

The composite faces cycled. Listening.

"They all chose something that wasn't you. That's who they are."

Seven seconds. Eight.

"You can't offer me mutual," Derek said, "because you don't know what mutual means. You have what they gave. You don't have what they kept."

Eleven seconds. Twelve.

Jenny called out from somewhere in the dark the entity couldn't reach, "Now, Derek."

Derek moved and the group moved with him. The entity, recalculating from the offer back to the pursuit, lost a half-second to the transition.

The half-second was enough.

Jenny emerged from the corridor junction without breaking pace, falling into step beside Derek. He looked at her. She looked at him. Neither asked if it worked; her presence was the answer.

Robert said something quiet that only Riley could hear. Derek didn't catch it. Whatever it was, she nodded once.

Then she said, to Carter, to the camera and to the people watching: "Chat, you've been with us all night. Stay with us for this part."

> StreamFan23: we're here.

> HauntHunter_Sarah: we're here.

> ShadowWatcher99: we're here.

> TechieTom [code: 9034]: we're here. all of us. counting.

Carter didn't add anything.

The group ran.

***

The loading dock opened around them like a held breath releasing.

Jenny's territory. Derek felt the difference in how she moved. Her shoulders dropped half an inch, stride lengthening, the specific confidence of someone who knew every bolt and shadow in a space. Her shelter was gone, cleared during the prep sequence hours ago, but her knowledge of it remained. She cut left without hesitation, angling them toward the north passage entrance.

Behind them, the entity entered the loading dock.

The space gave it room the corridor hadn't. It spread into the volume like something unfolding, the composite form finding its full dimensions for the first time since the convergence point. Derek heard the change; the grinding became lower, more resonant.

"North passage, twenty feet," Maddie called. "Straight through, door at the end."

Jenny stopped with the deliberate stillness of someone who had made a decision years in the making. She was looking at the east wall of the loading dock; a section Derek had never examined, the industrial green paint peeling over riveted steel plates. A mechanism. Original installation. Heavy, manual, and designed for hands that understood what leverage meant.

She turned to Derek.

"Get them through the door."

"Jenny—"

"I know this building better than anything left in it does." Her eyes moved past him to the entity, which was crossing the loading dock with unhurried certainty. "Go through the door, Derek. Now."

He looked at her and she looked back. The expression on her face was the specific calm of someone who had found the moment and was not going to waste it on goodbyes.

He turned.

"Move. Door. Now. GO."

The group moved. Carter, running backward, got one last frame of Jenny in the loading dock. Her hands reached for the mechanism on the east wall, combat boots planted on concrete she'd walked for years, facing the entity that was closing the distance between them.

The north passage swallowed them. Dark and narrow; the safe route. Jenny's route. Thomas's route. The route that had been the answer all night.

Behind them was the sound of heavy steel moving. Industrial. Mechanical. A loading dock safety seal engaging for the first time since 1927, designed to hold against chemical emergency forces.

Then the sound of the entity hitting the seal, once. The steel held.

> **StreamFan23:** *the dock doors are closing. she's still in there.*

> **ShadowWatcher99:** *jenny. jenny reeves. 1986 to tonight.*

> **CandyKid_98:** *jenny.*

Carter read CandyKid's single word aloud while running. The account flickered and went quiet again.

Derek kept running. The north passage stretched ahead: fifty feet, forty, thirty. The corrugated steel door sat at the end, the door they'd entered through. A different lifetime.

Then he felt it. The instinct that had been reading people all night: Robert was not at the door.

Derek turned. Twenty feet back, at a junction in the corridor that Derek didn't remember being a junction, Robert Morgan stood with his hand already reaching toward the floor. His lab coat caught the last of Carter's light. His posture was not the posture of someone running toward an exit.

"Robert—" Riley's voice, from ahead. She was through the door. She was outside. Her voice came back through it like something torn.

Robert didn't look up. "I told you in the dock. Go."

"Robert." Derek.

Robert looked up then, at Derek.

"This is the result I was looking for," he said. Then, quieter: "Go, son. I'll be all right."

He placed his hand on the floor and closed his eyes.

"The factory processes emotions." He said quietly. "It never understood them. That's always been its weakness."

The junction glowed. The air changed quality the way water changes when the temperature drops past a threshold. Derek felt it in his teeth.

> ***TechieTom [code: 9034]:*** *temporal signatures collapsing across the factory. every processed consciousness in the network is being released. the displacement is grounding the whole temporal layer. robert is*

> ***HauntHunter_Sarah:*** *he's going back. the displacement is grounding out. he's returning to 1963.*

> ***StreamFan23:*** *robert.*

The corridor emptied, and then the corridor was just a corridor. The building separation accelerated and Derek felt it in the floor beneath his feet.

> ***TechieTom [code: 9034]:*** *the temporal echo is grounding. building structural integrity compromised. derek you need to go RIGHT NOW.*

Derek went.

Through the door, into air that was cold and clean and smelled like nothing that had ever been processed. The gravel lot. The sky not black anymore; the dark blue that comes before dawn.

> *TechieTom [code: 9034]: derek is out. 10.*

> *TechieTom [code: 9034]: 9.*

> *StreamFan23: go go go go go*

> *TechieTom [code: 9034]: 8.*

> *HauntHunter_Sarah: MOVE.*

They ran. Five of them across the gravel lot — Carter, Evan, Maddie, Ava, Derek, Riley. Their flashlight beams were swinging wildly, the camera catching the building over Carter's shoulder. Derek didn't look back. His shoulder was registering the pain now, deep and specific, the contact from the convergence point finding its full voice without adrenaline to mute it.

TechieTom [code: 9034]: 5. 4. 3.

Ava stopped. She turned and raised the sketchpad in her left hand to document it: the building, in the moment before.

TechieTom [code: 9034]: 2. 1.

The Delightful Candy Company collapsed inward.

An implosion. The building came in on itself as the architecture that had held it operational for sixty years separated cleanly from the physical structure it was sustaining. The smokestacks folded, the corrugated steel entrance crumpled like paper. The loading dock with its sealed mechanism and whatever was still inside it went down into the foundation with a sound that traveled through the ground rather than the air. A single low thud that Derek felt in his knees.

The factory's pervasive, artificial, wrong sweetness. Gone, replaced by the smell of early morning, the smell of a field.

The gravel lot. Five people standing in it. The camera still running.

Carter turned the camera around. He didn't have a sign-off line. He didn't even have a summary.

"That's the stream."

He turned it off.

TechieTom [code: 9034]: you made it.

HauntHunter_Sarah: you made it.

StreamFan23: you made it.

ShadowWatcher99: you made it.

CandyKid_98: thank you.

The stream ended.

Derek stood in the gravel lot. His shoulder, he could feel it now, the deep bruise of something that would require imaging and probably weeks. Ava's hand had stopped bleeding at some point during the run; she didn't know when. She was holding the sketchpad in her left hand, not looking at the screen, not yet.

Riley was holding the journal. It had stopped writing. On its last page in Robert's handwriting, in ink that was still wet were two words: *Tell them.*

She pressed the journal to her chest. She didn't say anything.

Evan had Marcus's cam in his bag.

Maddie was counting. She was always counting. Five people. Five. The count was right.

"We should move away from it," she said. "Structural instability."

They moved. Nobody argued. They walked away from where the building had been. There was nothing behind them now.

They walked.

12

Riley pressed her back against the van's cold metal and held the journal shut.

The gravel lot was quiet in the way places are quiet after something enormous has stopped happening in them. That specific absence of noise, like the ringing after a concert, the ear still expecting the next beat.

Five-oh-something in the morning. The sky that shade of blue-black that meant dawn was coming but hadn't committed. Iridescent dust settled around them in slow spirals, catching the last of Carter's flashlight beam in colors Riley didn't have names for; somewhere between mother-of-pearl and oil slick, beautiful in the way things are beautiful when you don't want them to be. It coated the van, the gravel, their clothes. It tasted faintly sweet on her lips. Not the factory's sweetness.

She catalogued the group the way she'd learned to over twelve hours that felt like twelve years.

Derek beside Ava, his weight shifted left, shoulder held at an angle that said *worse than I'm telling you*. He hadn't said a word about it; Carter hadn't asked. Both of them were going to maintain this arrangement for exactly as long as it took someone else to break it. Ava's left hand was wrapped in Derek's jacket sleeve, the knot already darkening where it pressed against whatever had opened up during the escape. Her right hand held the sketchpad, screen angled away from Riley, and her face while looking at it was… something. Not shock. Something Riley couldn't read from this distance.

Evan opened his bag. Looked at the bodycam. Closed the bag. Opened it again. The factory couldn't touch it. He knew this. He was processing what it meant.

Carter sat on the van's bumper with the camera in his lap like a dead bird. He hadn't turned it back on. Riley had never seen him within arm's reach of a camera and not filming. The stillness of his hands was louder than anything he could have said.

Maddie's tablet glowed in the dark. Her fingers moved across the screen, archiving, preserving. Making sure the record survived the morning. She hadn't looked up once.

Riley traced her tattoo. The candy wrapper lines on her wrist, faded and familiar. Her great-grandfather had drawn that design. He'd drawn it as a warning and she'd turned it into ink and the ink had carried her here… and here was a gravel lot at five in the morning with dust on her clothes and a journal in her hands.

She didn't open it.

Instead she stood, walked to Ava. Crouched beside her.

"Let me see your hand."

Ava extended her left hand without looking away from the sketchpad. Riley checked the wrapping; Derek's work was tight enough, and holding. "You'll need stitches."

"I know." Ava's voice was quiet. Steady. "Riley, look at this."

Riley looked at the screen.

The sketchpad had generated something during the collapse. Autonomously while Ava ran, completing itself as the everything grounded out. What it showed was not the exterior implosion.

It showed the interior. The gaps.

Every processed person's absence rendered in Ava's visual language as the shapes of what they'd kept back. Thomas held his camera at an angle that said *I'm still filming this*. Clara with her clipboard, posture impeccable, data running down the page in handwriting so precise it was legible even as negative space. William at attention, the flashlight beam he carried cutting clean through whatever surrounded him. Michael with a wrench in his hand and oil stains running the wrong direction. Amber mid-scroll on a screen that wasn't there anymore, frozen in a pose that was half forum-post angle and half genuine surprise. Jenny with her feet planted. The combat boots and red laces. The specific stance of someone who had held ground.

Each gap was open; the implosion hadn't closed them.

"Ava," Riley said quietly. "Is that what I think it is?"

"I think so. Yes."

"Then Clara is free."

"I think they all are."

Riley stared at the clipboard, the posture, the jade pendant visible even in absence; she thought of CandyKid_98 typing into a chat room at five in the morning, waiting.

She pulled out her phone. The stream was offline but the chat platform was still active, 200,000 people who had become something during the night and hadn't stopped being it just because the broadcast ended. She scrolled.

CandyKid_98: is clara free

HauntHunter_Sarah: riley. ava. carter. evan. maddie. derek. are you all out. please say you're out.

TechieTom: i'm still monitoring. all factory signals are gone. external network analysis shows complete termination. i'm also still tracking those 23 devices. they're clearing. slowly. but clearing.

*StreamFan23: i closed the tab. i actually closed it.
i've been trying for hours and it closed.*

*ShadowWatcher99: my hands are shaking. is
everyone else's hands shaking.*

*NightOwl_Explores: sitting in my car outside my
apartment at 5am. cannot go inside yet. anyone else.*

*FilmNerd_404: thomas martinez. documentary
filmmaker. he would have loved this. all of us, here,
at 5am.*

Riley read the FilmNerd message twice. She typed, thumbs clumsy with cold and residue dust:

*We're out. All five. We're in the parking lot. We're
okay.*

She paused and looked down at the sketchpad in Ava's hand. At Clara's open gap.

Clara is free. I think they all are.

The chat responded immediately, overwhelmingly, too many messages to read individually. But one cut through:

*CandyKid_98: oh thank god. oh thank god. thank you.
thank you thank you thank you.*

Riley put the phone down. She sat back against the van's rear wheel beside Ava and Derek. The gravel was cold through her jacket and it was just gravel. Just ground. Not trying to do anything. Not processing anything.

She opened the journal.

Robert's handwriting filled the final pages. Entries that had written themselves during the night, ink appearing as he moved through the factory alongside them. She skimmed the middle pages. There were observations, warnings that had arrived too late to read and just in time to matter. Technical details she'd pass to Maddie later.

The last entry was written during the grounding, the ink still wet, smearing slightly under her thumb.

> *The factory processes emotions. It never understood them. That is its weakness and our persistent advantage. There are other factories. There have always been other factories. The people who stopped this one know how. The record is complete. Tell them.*

And below that, the pressure was lighter, the pen barely touching the page, as if he'd almost not written it.

> *She has her grandmother's eyes. I see it now.*

Riley sat with it. The gravel and the dust. The dark blue going lighter at the edges. He'd seen her. Across sixty years and one impossible night, he had looked at her and seen her grandmother and recognized his own blood and said goodbye in a way which was exactly, precisely who Robert Morgan was.

She passed the journal to Carter without speaking. He read it, then passed it to Evan. Evan to Maddie, who looked up from her tablet for the first time. Maddie to Ava. Ava to Derek. Derek read it last, one-handed, his right arm held carefully still.

He handed it back.

"What are you going to do with it?"

"What he said."

"Tell them?"

"Tell them."

Derek nodded. Looked at his shoulder, and then at Riley.

"Okay. But maybe after a hospital."

Carter made a sound that wasn't quite a laugh; the shape of one, he looked too tired and too relieved to produce the full version. Evan made the same sound half a second later. Ava concurred, softer, against the van's wheel.

Maddie glanced up from her tablet with the expression of someone who had been waiting for this moment and had prepared accordingly.

"The nearest emergency department with under forty-minute wait times is fourteen minutes from here." She paused, glasses catching the first real light of dawn. "I've been looking it up."

Nobody said Jenny's name. The absence sat in the gravel with them, present and unnamed.

***

Riley's coffee had gone cold an hour ago.

She knew this the way she knew most things about her apartment at ten on a Wednesday morning; peripherally, through some channel that wasn't quite attention. The mug sat at the edge of her desk beside Robert's journal, which was open to the page with the seven complaint filing numbers and beside her own journal, which was open to the page where she'd stopped writing three days ago mid-paragraph.

The paragraph was about Clara.

She'd been trying to describe what sixty years of keeping a record from inside a system designed to erase records looked like. She kept writing sentences deleting them because accuracy wasn't the problem. Every sentence about Clara contained Robert. They also contained the viewers and CandyKid_98 and Riley couldn't write all of them simultaneously even though they were all simultaneously true.

She picked up the pen. Put it down. Traced the tattoo on her wrist; the candy wrapper lines were uncovered now, her sleeves pushed up past the elbow. She'd stopped covering it the second week. It was hers; it had always been hers.

On her laptop, three tabs were open. The county records search she'd been running since Tuesday. A news archive from 1964 that contained exactly one paragraph about the factory's closure, attributed to "financial difficulties." And TechieTom's forum thread, which was forty-seven thousand words long this morning and had gained three new contributions since she'd last refreshed.

She refreshed again.

The new contribution at the top was from someone calling themselves LaborHistory_Researcher. Long post. Detailed. Riley read it twice, the second time slower.

> *Seven complaints. All properly filed. All closed with the same notation: 'Resolved — no further action pursuant to corporate discretion.' I've been cross-referencing the factory's employment records with contemporary labor dispute filings in four states. The notation is identical across facilities. Different companies. Different decades. Same language, word for word. I've found four other facilities with identical complaint closure language.*

Riley copied the link, opened her phone. Texted it to Maddie.

Maddie's response: three seconds. *"I know. I'm at number nine in the chain."*

Riley set the phone down and looked at the forum thread again. Scrolled past the labor historian's post to what sat beneath it; the thing she'd been reading, on and off, for three days.

TechieTom's entry from seventy-two hours ago. Flagged with the rolling verification code he still used. The entry documented a single forum post that had appeared at 3:47am:

***CandyMan_1963:** Documentation noted. Archive is incomplete. There are other records.*

TechieTom's analysis was characteristically precise: account network signature did not originate from the factory's terminated network. It originated from one of the twenty-three deep-processing devices. One of the three that had cleared in a way TechieTom described as "within parameters but qualitatively distinct from the other twenty." He did not know what it meant, he said so plainly.

Riley had a hypothesis. She was not ready to state it.

She turned back to the document she'd been writing, the one that wasn't the journal. It was the document that used Robert's records, Clara's quality control notes and the chat's compiled testimony. Also Sarah Thompson's preserved archive, released through the digital layer the termination sequence had freed. An account of the night at the Delightful Candy Company. A record. The first chapter of something longer that would name the seven complaints and who closed them and why, and what the closure notation meant across state lines and decades.

She was two paragraphs from where she'd stopped. She wrote one sentence. Deleted it. Wrote it again differently.

Her phone buzzed. A direct message. The notification showed CandyKid_98's handle.

Riley opened it.

> *I talked to my grandmother, who is 86. I told her what happened. About Clara. About the factory. About the stream.*

There was a pause. The typing indicator appeared and disappeared twice before the second message arrived:

> *She cried. She said: 'So she was there. She was there*

all along.' She'd always believed Clara didn't just disappear. That something had her. She was right.

Another pause, longer this time.

My grandmother asked me to thank whoever went in there. I told her it was a lot of people. She said thank them anyway. So. Thank you. From her.

Riley set the phone on the desk. She glanced over at Robert's journal; the entry that said *Tell them.* She looked at the forum thread where forty-seven thousand words of community documentation sat, growing daily, attributed and named., and then at the tattoo on her wrist.

She picked the phone back up. She typed:

Tell your grandmother Clara kept the record. From inside. Sixty years. She never stopped.

She sent it. She set the phone face-down on the desk.

The coffee was cold. The light through her window was the specific flat gold of mid-autumn morning, ten o'clock and ordinary. Outside, a Wednesday continued being a Wednesday. Someone's dog barked. A car door closed.

Riley picked up the pen. She turned back to the document. The paragraph about Clara that she'd been circling for three days, she wrote it now. Straight through, without stopping or deleting. Then the next paragraph. Then the next.

The last line she wrote before her hand paused:

The processing always depends on containment. The most important thing the record can do is refuse to be contained.

She read it back. She kept it.

She saved the document and sat back. Looked at the two journals side by side on the desk, one finished and one filling. The forum thread on her screen and its growing list of names. The message from CandyKid that she would read again tonight, later, when she had room.

She picked up her phone and opened the group text. She began to type.

> *I'm ready to talk about what comes next. When is everyone free?*
>
> *Maddie: Whenever. I have information.*
>
> *Evan: Evening works. Also I made a decision about the footage.*
>
> *Ava: I have things to show you. The app has been busy.*
>
> *Derek: PT ends at 4. After that.*

Carter's was last, after a pause that was longer than the others.

> *Yeah. Let's talk.*

Riley looked at Carter's message for a moment. Carter, who had turned the camera off, who had said *That's the stream* and meant it. Who hadn't posted anything in three weeks. Who was, apparently, ready.

She put the phone down. She picked up the pen. She kept writing.

***

The smell of garlic and something with rosemary hit Riley at the door. Carter in an apron, sleeves rolled to his elbows, a wooden spoon in his hand instead of a camera. He looked almost embarrassed about it.

"Derek already set the table," he said. "He's been here an hour."

"My PT ended early," Derek called from inside. "Also, your cutting board technique is terrible and I fixed it."

Riley stepped in. Carter's apartment was warm and too clean. The camera sat on the coffee table beside a small evidence bag containing Marcus's cam footage. Beside that, Ava's phone propped against a coffee mug. And on the TV screen above the couch, TechieTom's forum thread scrolled in real time. Forty-nine thousand words now. Still growing.

She set her document draft on the table and both journals beside it. The stack looked small for what it contained.

Evan arrived two minutes later, laptop bag over his shoulder, and Ava right behind him, her left hand still bandaged but the fingers moving freely. She'd been sketching with that hand for a week, she'd told Riley over text. Couldn't stop.

They ate. Carter's food was good; surprisingly, genuinely good. A chicken thing with lemon and herbs that he served without commentary, like he'd been cooking for years instead of three weeks. Derek made a joke about his sling that involved the phrase "factory-certified disability" and the table went quiet for half a second before Evan laughed, and then everyone did, and it was fine. .

After plates were cleared, they settled in the living room. The coffee table between them with its three objects: bodycam, phone, camera. Riley's document beside them.

Evan spoke first.

He looked at the evidence bag. "I've been thinking about this for three weeks. Marcus made it. His cam, his footage. The factory at full operational capacity." He paused. "There's a documentary film program at the university. They have a preservation unit. Chain of custody documentation. They'll hold it properly. With Marcus's name as primary creator."

He looked at Carter specifically. "Marcus made it. It belongs in a place that knows how to handle what he made."

Carter nodded once, he didn't argue. His hands stayed still in his lap, and Riley watched him not reach for the camera on the table. The nod was below commentary. Acceptance.

On the TV screen behind them, the forum thread updated:

> ***FilmNerd_404:*** *Marcus Johnson Urban Exploration Archive — someone should start this. His channel is still live. 40,000 subscribers. They're still watching.*

Riley watched Carter read it. He picked up his camera from the table; he just held it. Turned it over in his hands like a familiar weight he was relearning.

"I've been thinking about it," he said. "My stream archive. The 200,000-plus views, the comments section." He looked at Riley. "I've been thinking about leaving it up, like with Marcus," he gestured at the tv. "With documentation and the forum thread linked. With names." A beat. "Robert's name."

He glanced down at the camera in his hands. "I don't know if that's right. But I think it might be."

Riley met his eyes. "It's the record."

"Yeah." He put the camera back on the table. Left it there.

"Okay," Ava said quietly. "My turn." She picked up her phone. "The sketchpad app has been generating images. Every three to four days, I'm not prompting it. I'm not even opening the app; it runs and I find the results."

She turned the phone toward them. It was not what any of them expected.

Floor plans, eleven of them. Different buildings, different styles; one that looked industrial-era American, one that was clearly older, European maybe. But in each one, the same processing channel architecture was visible. The wrapper pattern. Robert's engineering diagram, functional and recognizable, threaded through spaces across decades and geography.

"Each image has location metadata embedded," Ava said. "I didn't put it there."

The room went quiet.

"The first one arrived the morning after," Ava continued. "I was still in the hospital waiting room. It matches a facility in Ohio." She swiped to the last image. "This one arrived yesterday. The metadata points to Scotland."

Maddie's name wasn't in the room but her work was. Riley pulled out her phone, opened the text thread. Read aloud: "The corporate chain goes international at number eleven. She thinks she knows what the app is drawing."

Derek leaned forward. His good arm on his knee, the sling holding the other still. He looked at the floor plans on Ava's screen. He looked at Riley's document on the table. He asked the thing none of them had said.

"So it's still running. Other versions of it are still running."

"That's what the record is for," Riley said.

"What does the record do against something that's been running since 1927?"

Riley looked at Robert's journal on the table. The leather cover, the pages that had written themselves during the worst night of her life. Seven complaints, one schematic. One secondary access point management didn't know about.

"It's what he had," she said. "It was enough."

Ava glanced down at the eleven floor plans on her screen. "The app isn't going to stop generating these."

"No," Riley said. "I don't think it is."

On the TV, the forum thread updated again:

> **HauntHunter_Sarah:** *Establishing a monitoring network — researchers who have documented similar facilities, who have lost people to them, who*

Riley read it. She picked up her pen. Wrote HauntHunter_Sarah's username in the margin of her document.

Derek sat back. The sling shifted against his chest. He looked around the room; at each of them, one by one.

"So we're doing this."

Not a question.

Nobody said *be careful.* Nobody said *are you sure.* Carter passed around seconds of the chicken. Evan explained the university archive's preservation protocols in more detail than anyone needed but nobody stopped him. Ava showed Derek how to zoom in on the floor plans with one hand. The forum thread grew by three posts while they talked.

Later, after Evan left with the evidence bag in his laptop case and after Ava and Derek walked out together still debating the architectural style of the Scotland image. After Carter stood at his door and said "same time next week?" like it was obvious, like they were a thing that met, Riley stood on the sidewalk in the dark and looked down at her wrist.

The tattoo, the candy wrapper lines in the lamplight from Carter's building. She hadn't covered it walking in and she wasn't covering it now. It was just there. Present. Hers in a way it hadn't been before she understood what it meant.

She walked to her car. She had a document to finish and a username to contact and eleven floor plans to cross-reference with Maddie's corporate chain. The work began tomorrow. The work had already begun.

The processing always depends on containment. The record refuses to be contained.

ABOUT THE AUTHOR

I.M. Knight's dark tales are steeped in the shadows of history. From a Christmas spent in a haunted Scottish castle to nights in ancient Roman nunneries, they've absorbed the whispers of centuries-old stones. Their explorations of London's Tower, Mayan ruins, and remote Pacific islands have taught them that every culture harbors its own terrors. Drawing from experiences in places where past and present blur - from Caribbean depths to Australian shores - Knight crafts psychological thrillers that probe the boundaries of human nature and identity. They write from Texas, where new shadows beckon.